Rockhaven
Spring

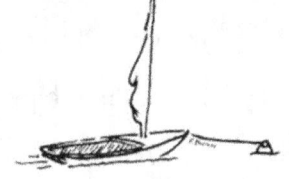

Farley Dunn

THREE SKILLET

ROCKHAVEN SPRING, Dunn, Farley L

First Edition

A Katie Carver Novel

 THREE SKILLET

www.ThreeSkilletPublishing.com

v.2

ISBN 978-1-943189-07-6

Enjoy all the Katie Carver novels:

Rockhaven Summer

Rockhaven Wedding

Rockhaven Christmas

Rockhaven Spring

Author's Note

Those of you familiar with Mid-Coast Maine will recognize elements of Vinalhaven Island in my Rockhaven series, but only because of my family history and the summers I've spent there. If you do visit Vinalhaven someday, look for Rockhaven. You'll find that magical place strewn all about the craggy shoreline and in the stalwart people that call Vinalhaven home.

1

"Look. Another Wyeth."

Katie Ragsdale and her friend Winnie Catron had said those words to each other a dozen times in the thirty minutes they'd been in the small gallery along the Maine coast.

Jeff, Katie's husband, had been more specific, wrapping his arms around his wife and whispering, "There, on that beach. I'd live there with you forever and ever and never miss the rest of the world." Once, he'd pulled her hair back on one side and kissed her on the neck, murmuring, "Andrew should have chosen you to sit for him. Then the paintings would have been worth twice as much."

"Thank you, Jeff. You might pay thousands of dollars for a painting of me, but no one else would." Katie had laughed.

"They're fools, then." Jeff, a minister at Rockhaven Town Church, chuckled. He was dressed in a warm overcoat, but he looked more lobsterman than preacher. He'd joined his wife to wish her best friend bon voyage after her extended visit over the Christmas holidays.

Just outside the plate glass windows fronting the gallery was the small mainland town that connected Rockhaven Island to the rest of the world, and it was filled with galleries and restaurants and wonderful storefront shops to entertain the casual visitor. This was their third gallery, and Jeff had said similar things to her in each one.

The women had moved on to a new painting, and Jeff leaned between them, pointing to a picture of a woman prominently displayed on one canvas. "You know, I delivered a mess of lobster to Betsy Wyeth on her island just south of here once."

"Betsy?" Winnie ran her finger along a postcard she'd picked up showing a group of Wyeth paintings all displayed on one wall. Each individual image was very small. She looked up with a smile, tilting her head to the side, and asked, "Who's Betsy?"

"Tell her, Jeff. Who's Betsy?" Katie wanted to hear this.

"If I must." He took a deep breath, running a hand through his flyaway hair, pulling it into place only until he released it. Jeff was indeed a lobsterman, and the sea kept his thick mop terminally unruly. "Andrew was one of the Wyeths, N.C., Andrew, and Jamie, three generations of a local family that are considered the First Family of American Art."

"And Betsy?" Winnie, still smiling brightly, fanned herself with yet a different one of the postcards.

"Yes, Jeff. Tell us about Betsy." Katie fought a laugh as she grabbed Winnie's arm. The postcard was creating a breeze.

"Betsy is, well, was Andrew's wife." Jeff grinned. "But everyone knows them around here. Ladies, we need to make sure we keep an eye on the time." He pulled his sleeve up to glance at his watch, rubbing his thumb across the face and frowning at it.

"They're divorced?" Winnie looked confused.

"He's being silly. I think she's his widow, right Jeff?" Katie reassured her friend. Then she turned to Jeff, placing two fingers on his chest. "And don't you worry, Preacher Man. My phone alarm's set."

Winnie was headed back to her home in Boston. Jeff's lobster boat was moored at the city wharf, but Katie had brought her car over on the ferry. The trip to the airport was only about ten minutes, so they were doing okay on time, but Katie was willing to admit that they might need to start thinking about heading that direction. They could not afford to be late.

"If you want that, you have to pay for it." Katie tapped the card in Winnie's fingers. "Which painting does it show?"

"Oh, I don't know." Winnie flipped it to the back and squinted. "Monhegan, I think. What's Monhegan?"

"Jeff?" Katie took the card and held it for him to see. It showed a house on a windswept island.

9

"One of the Wyeths owns that house. Monhegan is the name of the island. Buy this, and you'll own a piece of it." He chuckled.

"You'll own a postcard." Katie held it back out to Winnie.

"I like it. Thank you, Jeffie. I can't believe that family painted all these. They should have used a phone, like me. It would be so much easier."

"They didn't have phones when most of these were painted. Not cell phones, anyway." Katie wrapped an arm in her friend's, as she picked out one of the post-cards for herself. "Look, for Cousin Nikki. This one's pretty. I can just send it to my old Boston apartment. I'm glad she's living there."

"I am, too, but I don't know about that picture, Sweetie. My phone does better pictures that that." She had her phone out, and she scrolled through to show a number of pictures she'd taken while on the island.

"Your phone's not a painting, and pictures you've taken aren't worth half-a-million dollars."

"Oh . . . they're worth how much?" Winnie's eyes were round, and she giggled. "If I had that for every picture I've posted on Facebook, I'd have a lot of money." She checked the time on her phone. "Forty minutes until my flight."

"I'll have you there. You put that phone away. Trust Katie. Katie is your friend. Katie is good. Katie is wise." She said it like a hypnotist, and she laughed.

"How small did you say the plane would be?" That was something that had concerned Winnie when Katie scheduled the flight. There was an issue with the amount of luggage returning to Boston with her. She'd ridden up with Cousin Nikki in a massively long limousine. Weight hadn't counted, then.

"Six seats. Quit worrying about it and enjoy the Wyeths. You won't find a collection like this just anywhere. The Wyeth family is local for three generations, so this is their home." Within fifty miles of Rockhaven was what she meant, but anyone homegrown would already know that. "You know Grandmamma had a Wyeth, once. It would have been worth a lot, now."

"Oh, Sweetie!" Winnie dropped her phone back into her bag and hugged Katie with one arm. "The fire. I'm so sorry."

A late-season fire had consumed Katie's childhood summer home on Rockhaven many years earlier. Katie's grandmother hadn't survived, and an empty foundation was all that was left.

"I don't remember a Wyeth at your grandmother's place." Jeff had spent much of his summers there as well when they were kids, in and out of the house with Katie and all their friends.

"No, no. I wasn't clear." Katie laughed. "It was at her place in Boston. No one knew what it was, and it went in a tag sale when my parents liquidated her estate."

"You poor baby. Are you still sad?" Winnie patted Katie's face with one hand.

"I barely remember it. Let me see if they have it here." Katie scanned the display and pulled a postcard out of the rack. It was the one showing the series of paintings on a wall, and she pointed to the smallest image. "There it is. That one. I might buy this. Just think, I'll own a Wyeth again." She chuckled.

"You'll own a postcard. Let me see." Jeff looked it over, flipping it to the back. "This would have been worth tons. Shame."

They paid for their postcards and braced for the stiff breeze that had driven them into the galleries in the first place. Once outside, the sky was a brilliant blue laced with wind-softened doilies, and a seabird with wide, white wings squawked at them before landing across the street to pick at something along the curb. Small strips of snow tried to hide in the shadowy areas along the foundations of buildings, reminding pedestrians and drivers alike that winter had a lot of oomph left in it, and not to trust the sun. Elsewhere, the sidewalks and roads were clear. Katie and Winnie wore borrowed hooded coats, with faux fur around the face. The coats had been left by Katie's Cousin Nikki when she departed for Boston two weeks earlier. For a bone-chilling winter day? They were perfect. For style? They screamed over-the-top Nikki.

"How are you holding up?" Jeff had his arm around Katie, his own rugged coat bulky against the cold breeze.

"Okay." She knew what he was asking. Three-and-a-half months along, and she'd lain in bed with her fair share of morning sickness. "Today's been good so far, and I wouldn't miss seeing Winnie off for anything."

"The cold. How's that working?"

"It settles my stomach." It did, too. It was the ferry

12

ride that had given her more problems. Hopefully, the return trip would be better. Eating? Until she got home, food was not an option.

A horn sounded. In the direction of the ocean, the ferry plowed through the harbor, leaving whitewater boas in its wake, heading out to sea. The car deck was mostly empty, with the bulk of the boat being swallowed by a gravel truck.

"Someone's getting a new driveway," Katie commented.

"Sweetie, look at this." Winnie tugged Katie's arm, and she pointed across the street.

"At what?" Katie followed the finger. It led to an antiques shop with an old-fashioned footed child's crib in the shop's window. She looked at Jeff and rolled her eyes.

Jeff shrugged and grinned, whispering, "She's your friend."

"Honey, not baby stuff." This was what Katie didn't want, people to fawn over her just because she'd announced on Christmas Day she had a little one on the way. She also didn't need reminded of the ferry ride back with her stomach. Not today. And anything baby would do just that.

"It's too cute. Can I go inside and get it for you?" Winnie clapped her hands in excitement as she stepped off the curb and started across the street. "Then I can post pictures of my little nephew in it and see how many likes I get."

"Having a baby's more than a Facebook photo op. I will have to raise this kid, and she might be a girl."

The crib was cute, but practical? Not by modern safety standards.

"Or it might be a boy. I like the word nephew." Jeff chuckled, calling out, "He'll be your nephew, Winnie. Keep your fingers crossed."

"Oh, you two." Katie knew it was hopeless, and she gave in. "We have a few minutes if you want to go inside."

"Thanks, Sweetie." Winnie beamed, and she pulled the door wide, laughing when an old-fashioned cow bell jangled to announce their entrance.

It was warm inside, and it smelled good, too, pine needles or perhaps a hint of eucalyptus. Old wood and the faint smell of decay suggested age. Weathered buoys, rush-bottomed chairs, and paintings—probably prints, Katie surmised—lined the walls. Winnie drew her directly to the old crib in the window.

"Ladies? May I help you?" An elderly man, nattily dressed, pushed through a curtain from a back room.

"My friend's catching a flight to Boston. She wanted to stop in and look at your crib." Katie pointed to it. Jeff had abandoned them when they passed the wall filled with old lobster buoys.

"Ah, the crib. Beautiful workmanship from the forties. Hand built. It would make a wonderful decorative piece." He stepped to the window and rocked it gently. "I'm Quincy Sorensen, proprietor. Do you collect dolls?"

"We're having a baby." Winnie's eyes followed the movement of the crib. She laughed, her strawberry blonde hair bouncing with the back and forth movement of her head. When the crib slowed, she laughed again and grasped Katie by the shoulders, calling out, "My friend is, anyway. I'm going to be an aunt."

"Ah, I'm afraid I can't help you there. This is a decorative piece only, nothing more. I can't sell it for use as an actual crib. I do have some old baby things over here that would be wonderful as display accessories, excellent in a baby's room." He smiled engagingly, indicating an alcove off the back wall of the room.

"Thank you, but no thanks." Katie smiled at him as she squeezed her friend's arm. She whispered to Winnie, "It was a good idea. Thanks, Honey. Maybe Jeff can build us one."

Something dinged, and Katie reached in her purse. Her phone glowed, and she dropped it back in. "Jeff, we have to go. Thank you, Mr. Sorensen. My friend's flight calls."

"Ah, come back again, anytime." He reached a hand to shake.

"This was fun. Thank you, Quincy." Winnie grabbed his hand with both of hers and pumped it vigorously. "Bye, bye!"

Jeff joined them underneath the dangling bell as they exited the store.

The car ride to the airport was barely five minutes, but unloading Winnie's luggage took three times that. The terminal was little more than a white building with a stretch of tarmac behind it, so Jeff served as the skycap to help them check in.

Before Winnie boarded, she hugged Jeff and thanked him for taking such good care of Katie. When

15

she hugged Katie, she said more.

"I love you so much, Sweetie. I'll miss you forever, but I promise to come back and see you."

"Be sure to visit Nikki. And you behave on all those shoots. I want to see you in my new catalogs." Katie felt her eyes burn. It was suddenly very real to her just how much she enjoyed her friend's exuberant lifestyle and her funny stories about the modeling gigs she attended all over the world. She already looked forward to her visiting again.

"I will, Sweetie. I'll keep you posted on Nikki, and I'll take you with me on every shoot I do. Now, a second hug for little Jeffie." She giggled at that and patted Katie's tummy, before hugging her again.

Jeff laughed and shook his head.

Giving Katie an extra hug, Winnie whispered, "Don't you worry about all that bad stuff they said about your grandmother's place out there on the Point. They built Venice on muddy islands. You've got solid rock. You can build whatever you want." Winnie waved and headed out the doors to climb into the aircraft.

"You heard that, Dame Carver. You can build whatever you want." Jeff had his arms around her, and they watched Winnie disappear inside with a wave.

Katie laughed his words off, but they had read the report that the existing foundations of her grandmother's old house were unstable. It had certainly put a kink into their plans to rebuild. The old design was grandfathered in, as long as Katie rebuilt on the same footprint. To have an architect draw up something completely new? Well, that was more difficult.

As the small plane taxied down the runway and lifted into the air, Katie and Jeff stepped to her car, and they climbed in. "Lunch, maybe, if you feel like eating?" Jeff took her hand.

"I want to, but I'm wearing down. I'm sorry."

"You're not sick, are you? I can call someone. A doctor. Do you need a doctor?" He pressed one of her hands to his face.

"Silly, of course I don't need a doctor. I need to stay off my feet for a while. The ferry ride will give me a chance to do just that." That wasn't how she'd felt earlier, but maybe it would be true this time. Reaching to the dash, she pulled down Winnie's postcard of Monhegan. "That Winnie," she said. "She couldn't even remember to take her postcard with her."

"Look on the back. I suspect she meant to leave it." Jeff touched it with one finger to peer at the underside.

Katie flipped it over to see a message in her friend's elaborate handwriting.

"Au revoir. (I got that from Nikki. It means goodbye for now.) I will miss you so much, Sweetie. All my love forever, Winnie."

Katie wiped the tears from her eyes, and she put the postcard back on the dash. As Jeff started the engine and headed the direction of the ferry, she was certain of one thing. Winnie, in spite of her many flaws, knew how to make her feel loved, and that was why she was the dearest friend she'd ever known.

"Was it a good message?" Jeff looked at her as he

17

turned the corner towards the ferry. "I'm headed back out on my boat, and I don't want you riding the ferry alone and miserable." He grinned and tapped her chin with his fingertips.

"The best, Jeff. I've enjoyed her visit very much."

"More than you enjoy me?"

"Hey, now, you are a funny man." She laughed, but she especially enjoyed the feel of his hand in hers all the way to town.

"Nina!" Katie rolled the glass down, calling to the heavily bundled form looking across the water from the car deck. It was the coat she recognized more than the person. Outside, in winter, on the ferry? The clothes made up half of who the person was. You learned to recognize people by fabrics and the cut of their clothing, or you didn't know them at all.

This was a coat worn by Nina Vinson, the proprietor of Harbor View restaurant, one of the few and the best on Rockhaven.

The coat turned, and Nina's face appeared. She lifted an arm, and pulling her hood tighter, she moved toward the car. "Katie! How are you doing, girl? Thank goodness the ferry hasn't pulled out, yet. I'd have been inside trying to warm up. Jeff told me you were bringing Winnie over today and to look for you on the way back."

Nina had leaned over, and she was speaking through about a three-inch gap in her hood opening.

"It's warm in here if you want to join me." Katie looked forward to visiting with Nina on the 75 minute ferry ride, but as importantly, she needed her friend inside. Katie could only run the engine until the ferry took off, and she needed the window up, or the car would be unbearable by the time they were to the island.

Nina glanced at the back of the ferry, and she laughed. "Sure. I have some things in the car, but they're as safe without me as with. Thank you. Doors unlocked, please." She tapped the locking button on the top of Katie's door, and ran towards the opposite side.

Katie tapped the unlock switch just as Nina's hand hit the handle.

"Ah," Nina breathed, as she pulled the door to. "I keep recommending electrical outlets on the car deck. It'd be worth it to me to have an electric heater wired into my car. Then I could run it on days like this."

"You look warm enough." Katie wrapped her hand around Nina's wrist—still in the coat—and squeezed. She couldn't find her friend's arm inside.

"Window dressing. This is January, in Maine, and all the bundling in the world can't keep a body completely warm. Now, you. I hear there's been an engineer out to your place on the Point. Have you received the results, yet?" Nina threw her hood back, and she began to unbutton the front of her coat. Her gloves remained on her hands.

"Let me show it to you." Katie reached into the back seat just as the ferry horn blew. The boat began to move, and the car shifted, sliding a large flat envelope out of Katie's grasp.

"Key, girl." Nina tapped the key in the ignition. "We're moving."

"Right." Katie chuckled and reached to kill the car. She leaned into the back seat again, this time barely touching the envelope with her fingertips. Pulling it forward, she slipped out a letter, and held it out. "Read this."

"Here, so," and Nina scanned down, keeping track with a finger, and occasionally stopping to read in detail. She flipped through several attached pages, one that showed the existing foundations, and another that showed buildable parameters that cut off one end of the old house. At the last page, she looked up. "All that money only to find the fire weakened the foundation walls, and they won't hold a new structure up? That I understand, but there was a house there before. Why can't it be reconstructed in the same spot, even if you replace the existing foundation?"

"A flaw in the bedrock. That isn't in the paperwork, but it seems Grandmamma was fortunate the original house never fell down. The old foundation walls are already pulling apart right where that line's drawn. It would seem the engineers actually know what they're talking about."

"For once." Nina chuckled. "What are your plans, now?"

"We feel stuck. It's a little disappointing, but at least we have the sleeping cabin." Katie shrugged as she slipped the engineering report back into its envelope. It was more than a little disappointing. Jeff had seemed as devastated as she felt, but there was nothing to be done about it, not in the middle of January. "It's not like the Point is five hours away. We can run out there in thirty minutes anytime we want. Who needs a real bathroom?"

The cabin didn't have one.

"You do know Kent and I bought a little place on Settler's Island about three years ago. Nothing much, little more than a primitive camp, with one room downstairs, and a loft that holds a bed." Nina smiled expectantly, as if that changed everything.

"You?" Katie laughed. "You live on an island, Rockhaven, and you have a vacation spot on an island, Settler's, that you can see just across the channel. What happened to Key West, or Hawaii?"

"Settler's Island is convenient. It's not the distance, it's the change of pace. And on Settler's, we can go every weekend, if we want."

"Where . . . I mean, where on Settler's? I might know it." Katie had sailed around Settler's numerous times as a girl. She hadn't been a girl for years, but still, she remembered every house that had been along the coast.

"No, you wouldn't have seen this one. It was empty land when we found it, all we could afford. Kent and I hauled the supplies ourselves and put it up. It's basic, but it's like magic to be there." Nina took a deep breath and smiled, as if enjoying the memory of it very much.

"You really love it, don't you?"

"Yes. You and Jeff? You need that place on the Point. Your baby needs it. So, what's the plan?"

Katie looked out her window and laughed. There was no plan, not with the engineer's report dashing dreams of her family home being rebuilt. Her generous Cousin Nikki had offered to provide the funds, but since replacing her grandmother's home was out the window, perhaps she'd change her mind. That was the real issue, and Katie and Jeff didn't know if the original design from a century earlier could be approved even in another location without the existing foundations as part of the grandfather clause. Building requirements had changed a lot over the past century.

So, what's the plan? Katie smiled. That question was one she'd asked an island boy from her church before Christmas. He had younger brothers who still believed in Santa, but he no longer did. Katie had convinced him not to spoil the moment for his brothers by coming up with a plan for Christmas, and things had gone every bit as smoothly as she'd hoped.

For her own problems, she had no plan at all. She turned when Nina cleared her throat.

"So, is there a plan?" Nina looked at her expectantly.

"Not yet. We're still working out this engineering report." She held the envelope up and laughed.

"I'll tell you, girl, what I'd do if I owned that property. I'd toss that report—" She took it from Katie and flipped it into the back seat. "—and I'd get me an architect on the phone. Send in the engineer's report, and find out what you can build. You might be surprised."

"It wouldn't be my grandmother's house." Katie sighed. She had long ago resigned herself—and quite happily—to using the property without the house being there. She and Jeff could be content with the sleeping cabin as a daytime getaway. It was her second cousin's unexpected offer to rebuild it that had stirred up the old longings again.

The ferry hit a rough patch in the water, and Katie felt her stomach churn. No, she thought. It's afternoon. I cannot be having morning sickness here. Behave, baby!

"Two things." Nina took Katie's hand in her gloved one. "One, never ride the ferry when you're pregnant. I saw that look. Second, this new house, if you rebuild, will be yours and Jeff's. The memories you make for your little one out there? The style of the house doesn't matter. Only the love that fills it is important. Now, you sit quietly, and you'll feel better by the time we get to the landing. Me, I've got to get ready to change cars." Nina pulled her coat around her, and she occupied herself with buttoning it.

"You're sweet, Nina." Katie smiled.

"Practical. Kent says it's the same thing, but thank you." She didn't look up.

Katie smiled again and turned to her window. However, Nina's reassuring words hadn't stopped her stomach from churning, and she didn't want to leave frozen stomach waste on the ferry deck for the entire island to see. Everyone would know. She tried to distract herself by imagining what a different style house on Carver Point might look like. Two stories or one? Lots of glass, or did she want clerestory windows and imaginative openings in interesting locations? A garage. Her grandmother had always wished for a garage. A full basement for rainy weather, a place to hang sheets and towels to dry. And, would she rent it? Many people on the island did, to cover expenses such as utilities and taxes. If so, that would need to be considered in the design.

Then it hit her. Taxes! Katie rubbed one temple with the tip of a finger. Cousin Nikki hadn't thought of that. If Carver House were replaced, taxes on the property would skyrocket. With the car payment Katie had brought from Boston, and no job on the island, money was not exactly flowing from the kitchen taps.

As they rounded the headland into Rockhaven Harbor, catching a swell much harder than normal, Katie's little Beetle jerked. Her stomach jerked, too, and she knew she couldn't hold this one back. She grabbed for the handle and opened the door; and leaning out as far as she could, she lost what little she had inside.

Nina tapped her arm when she was finished. "You pay no mind. They have cleaner for that. I've got to get to my car, though. I've enjoyed my visit. Think about that house, and let me know what you and Jeff decide. It might be fun." Then she was out the door and gone.

As Katie wiped her mouth, she saw Nina pointing

out the mess to one of the ferry attendants, and before the ship hit the landing, he already had an absorbent covering the spill.

Baby, come quickly, Katie moaned, as she pulled forward and off the ferry. She had no idea it would be like this. Carver House? Who cared, when little Ragsdale was at war with her insides.

3

The beveled glass in the front door clattered as it closed, bringing Katie awake. The room swam when she tried to sit.

"Katie, honey?" Jeff called to her.

"On the sofa." She let her head drop and raised a hand like a periscope. "It's not a good day."

"Will this make it better?" He sat on the coffee table and took her hand. With a smile, he lifted it to his lips and kissed it. "Any improvement?"

"It's my stomach, not my hand that hurts. Baby exhaustion. I should trademark that phrase." She laughed, enjoying the attention. Jeff smelled good. Ocean good. He'd been out on his boat, and he still wore his weatherproof gear. "If I write a book about baby exhaustion and how to get through it, then I'll never have to work again, and we'll have plenty of money."

"I have you. I don't care about the money. What can I do for you?" He pressed her hand against the side of his face.

"Have this baby. All I did was run Winnie to the airport, and I'm wiped out. How could a baby sap so much of my energy?"

It was more than that, though. It was the house she couldn't get clean, the car she'd kept that Jeff didn't really have the money to pay for, and his talk of selling his Jeep. He loved that Jeep, with its ragtop and four giant tires, and she didn't want him to be forced to give it up.

She'd never considered how the year-rounders survived on Rockhaven. As a girl, being a summer person, she'd just assumed they did. However, besides lobstering, how many jobs were there on the island? Not many, she was finding.

ALDMass, take me away! She laughed to herself as she looked into Jeff's eyes, and enjoyed the touch of his skin against hers. She'd gone so far as to send an email to Connie Rivera, her old boss, asking information about doing piecework for the company. If she could work from home . . . but she'd received no answer back, yet.

"If I get us something to eat, will you have energy to listen to the latest news?" Jeff fought a smile. It was clear he had something big to tell.

"I can listen. Just tell me." She wanted to smile back, but that took energy. The baby had all of hers.

"No. Food first." He stood and went to the window

28

and looked out over Moffat Cove. "The boat's running well. That cough from last week hasn't come back. See? A little prayer goes a long way. Now, though. Food. What'll you have? Yesterday's chicken soup, or a fresh BLT?" He turned from the window and smiled.

"Bring me what you like. It'll probably come back up, anyway." Thinking back, she'd felt fine before the ferry ride back from the mainland, and no, she hadn't eaten since losing everything. Being hungry might be part of the problem. She struggled to a sitting position and put her feet on the coffee table. "Beans, do we have any of those? Chili and beans, and a Coke. The real thing, with caffeine and sugar."

"Real chili? From scratch?" Jeff didn't sound sure about that.

"Yes, from scratch. Out-of-the-can scratch. There should be one left on the shelf beside the fridge."

"Yes, ma'am, Dame Carver." He grinned and saluted, and headed into the kitchen.

That made Katie smile, like everything would work out fine. It was a private endearment that no one else understood, a connection to her return from the island the summer before after a fourteen-year hiatus, and finding Jeff still in love with her, still waiting on her, and giving her the opportunity to discover she was still in love with him. He had teased her with those words, and she had bristled; now they had become part of a bond that linked them as surely as life on Rockhaven was linked to the sea.

"What's the latest news?" She called it loudly to get over the noise in the kitchen.

"Oh, it's Ritchey." The words came to her, filtered through the doorway. "Work's moving ahead on the shop."

"The empty storefront? The one on Main?" That surprised her. Not that Ritchey, Jeff's friend from their teen years, had anything to do with the shop, but that it was happening now. The sun might have been out all day, but winter still had Maine firmly bundled up and wishing for spring.

"You didn't see when you were in town today?" Jeff stood in the doorway with a pan in his hand, and he scraped the sides with a large spoon. "A truck came in on the 1:00. Isn't that the one you were on?"

"I didn't notice. Sorry. Nina was there, and she joined me in the car for a visit. I never got out." She remembered how the wind had cut her skin when she had the window down. Then she'd begun to feel ill, and she hadn't cared who else was on the boat.

"Ah. It was a box truck, anyway, so you wouldn't have been able to tell. It was unloading at the new store when I was dropping off today's catch at Orren's wharf." Orren Swears handled Jeff's daily catch for a percentage. "They were taping brown paper over the insides of the windows. The delivery truck had the street blocked, so I'll bet Archie Coombs raises a complaint at the next town meeting. If we want to eat, I'd better get this on the stove." He raised the pan to show Katie, then he laughed and turned back into the kitchen.

"I like Archie." Katie didn't know him well, but he seemed nice enough. He'd been to services at Rockhaven Town Church once, and he'd smiled when he greeted her. She'd asked if he had an email address so she could send him her weekly sermon notes, and he'd guffawed, telling her that email was for city folks. He'd put in a phone line forty years before, and no one called him on that. Why would they send him an email? He'd chuckled as he walked away, getting into an old van that looked more rust than rusty, and started it up in a cloud of blue smoke.

"So, Archie has a fan." Jeff's amusement could be heard in his words. "Good for you, Katie. More people should be like you, able to find the good in people."

"Is that so?" She leaned her head back and closed her eyes, sinking into the building drowsiness that seemed ready to consume her day. It wasn't worth fighting any longer. She heard the oil heater click three times, and the fan began to blow. Pulling a throw from the end of the sofa, she covered herself and tucked it under her chin. She smiled at the touch of a kiss on her cheek.

"You look comfy. Can I join you?" Jeff whispered the words to her.

"You can bring me food." She took a deep breath, and she smiled again, filled up with her love for this man who treated her so well. She smelled food, too, and her stomach grumbled. Real grumbles, not nausea flip-flops, and for that, she was grateful.

"Said and done. Open your peepers."

Katie looked to see a steaming bowl of chili in front of her, seated in a second bowl lined with a paper towel. They were on a plate with four crackers to the side. When she took it, Jeff produced a Coke in a bright red can, and he set it on the table at the end of the sofa.

"Oh, Jeff, I think I can survive the day." She spooned up a bite of the chili, and she bit into a chunk of meat. The flavor exploded into her mouth. "This is the best thing I've ever tasted. Hand me that drink, please."

"Better than Thanksgiving turkey?" He teased with a twinkle in his eye.

"Even better than pumpkin pie, but don't tell Roker that." Roker was Jeff's friend on the island, although he had quickly become a good friend of Katie's, also. Roker's favorite pie was pumpkin, especially when prepared by Jess up on High Road.

"My lips are sealed." Jeff drew a conspiratorial finger across his mouth, "zipping" his lips together. "You, my beautiful woman, enjoy your chili and beans, because I want you to get to feeling better. We need to head out to the Point later."

"The Point? Today?"

"Today. I have something very special to show you." His expression said that's all he was going to say.

"It'll be closing in on night by the time we get there." She was feeling better, though. Beans, chili, and caffeine were proving just the thing. As her doctor had instructed her when she told him that she didn't feel like eating when she was nauseous, whatever gets food and water into her system was better than dehydration and starving the baby.

"I remember a time when I would have looked forward to it being dark." Jeff's eyes crinkled in barely controlled laughter.

"Not anymore?" She was teasing, and that told her she was definitely feeling more like her old self. She dipped up the last of the chili and held out the bowl to him.

This time Jeff laughed aloud. "Now, you never heard me say that. I'm always happy to be in the dark with you."

Katie watched him walk away, and she felt of her belly, thinking, And look where it's got us now. She didn't mind, though, at least not most days. However, for the next six months, she was staying off the ferry, unless someone was dying. Puking was not fun, and that's where Katie drew the line.

She did let Jeff help her stand and put on her coat. She was grateful it still fit around her waist, and maybe spring would come before the baby got too big. She couldn't afford a new one, not unless she heard from ALDMass with some very good news.

Having a baby on a Maine island. In the winter. What an experience this was turning out to be!

4

"Jeff, is that Kevie?" A boy trudged beside the road about a quarter mile in front of them, headed the same direction. "I know that walk. It is. Stop up here, and let's see what he's doing."

Kevie was Al and Janine Peavey's eldest of four. He was the boy Katie had convinced to go along with Christmas for his younger brothers a month back. He held something oddly shaped in one hand.

Jeff chuckled, glancing in his mirror. "We've got company coming up, but I think we're good." Good to stop beside Kevie, he meant. The "company" was a car a good distance behind them. "You can tell it's Kevie from his walk?"

He had a point. The boy had on a thick coat, a hood pulled over his head, and mittens on his hands. As they grew closer, he turned to wave, and his face was wrapped with a muffler. They could barely see his eyes.

"Don't you watch people? Of course I can tell." Katie pointed. "Pull over here."

"Sure, I watch people, but usually their faces." He teased her. "I don't recognize anyone's backside."

He forced the four-wheel-drive machine into a lower gear, and the engine roared as they slowed to a crawl. He applied the brakes as he eased two wheels off the road. The car coming up gave a warning honk, then pulled to the opposite lane and sped up to go around.

"Kevie? Do you need a ride?" Katie had the window cracked, and she called out through the opening as Jeff rolled to a stop.

"Hi, Miss Katie. Hey, Jeff." He waved with his free hand. His voice was muffled through all the fabric. "Nah. I'm fine. Besides, I've got this, and I need to carry it outside." His eyes crinkled, and it was clear he was smiling.

"How was school today?"

"Fine. Konnar had to sit in the corner." His eyes were crinkled again. Konnar was one of his brothers.

"I'll bet he was embarrassed." Katie expected Kevie had done his best to make sure of it, and she was certain Konnar would do the same at the first opportunity.

"He wasn't embarrassed. He was just stupid. Everyone kept asking me why he was in the corner. I told them it was the stupid corner, and Konnar has to sit there for the rest of the year."

"Kevie!" Katie fought to keep from laughing. "Come on and get inside." She motioned with her hand.

"I would, but—" He held up the package.

"We don't mind. What is it?" Katie rolled the window down more, noticing that the heater fan had turned up a notch. She rolled the window down farther. "We have plenty of room."

"Nah. Mom said I can't let anyone pick me up. I better get on. I've got a long way to go. Bye!" He waved again, and turning his back to them, he started down the side of the road.

"What was that about?" Katie rolled her window up. "Janine is making him walk outside in this?"

"He's thoroughly insulated. I don't think you have to worry that an eleven-year-old will freeze on Rockhaven. Kids here know better." Jeff worked the transmission into first, and he pulled back onto the road. As they passed the boy, he honked twice. "Once for each of us."

"In Boston, they'd chase you down and shoot a gun at you for that."

"For what? Stopping to offer a ride to a good friend's kid?" Laughter was twisted in Jeff's question, telling how absurd he found that. He picked up her hand and kissed it. "What about if it's a pretty girl? One I'm married to? Can I stop and give her a ride?"

"You are so silly. I'm glad I married you." Katie refused to let go of his hand, even when he pushed the lever into a new gear. She liked touching him, any part of him. It filled her with satisfaction in a way that

36

nothing else could.

"Tell me, why is someone planning on shooting out my back window?"

"The honking thing. Up here, people pass and they honk. That's strange." She shivered.

"Only if you're not a Rockhavener. And all of us aren't strange, you know. Only those with broken horns. We think they're the strange ones, because they don't honk at us." He laughed. They were passing the Town Park, where the gazebo that had caught fire just before Christmas still showed damage on one side. It wouldn't get repaired until warmer weather, though. As Jeff had told Katie when she asked about it, nothing outdoors got repaired in winter in Maine, not unless it was urgent. It was too much trouble arguing with Mother Nature, because Mother Nature almost always won.

"The truck's gone." They had reached Main, with Rockhaven Harbor to the left, and Ritchey Hickox's empty and very raw storefront to the right. "Slow down. I want to look."

Vast sheets of brown paper covered the windows of the old building, just as Jeff had said. It, as did everything on Main Street, dated from the heyday of Rockhaven over a hundred years before. The double-glazed glass walls fronting the road were newer, and the piers holding the backside up over the saltwater pond that flooded under Main street at the turn of every tide had been replaced more than once, but a casual visitor would only see age and character.

It was why Katie knew it was a perfect location for

Ritchey to branch out with his sporting goods chain of stores. It was as exciting as it was surprising to see progress already happening in the middle of January. No one had expected to see anything going on inside the building until March, at the earliest.

"Okay, Starry-Eyes, what are you seeing?" Jeff pointed to the roof. "Ritchey must be doing well. There. The heat's on." Above the building steam rose from a vent. "Either that or they've already turned the water on. If so, they'll have to run the heat from here on out. I'd hate to pay his heating bill."

"Yeah," she said. She was thinking, though. ALDMass. Ritchey's store, whatever he decided to call it. Ideas flashed through her head, and she tried to catalog them away. She was distracted by Jeff.

"Are you ready to head out?" Jeff squeezed her hand.

"Sure." She glanced at a sign in the window. Construction Permit Approved. There was more underneath, but the words were too small to read.

"Then we're off." Jeff took the shifter and pushed it into neutral, rocking it back and forth, and he looked behind them. Then, with the clutch depressed, he slipped it easily into first. Before he could pull forward, Katie put her hand on his.

"Not too fast, Jeff. I'm feeling better, but I won't be well for another five and a half months. Speed is not what I need."

"Okay, my little turtle. I'll creep along at your side. Can I do a fast creep? I'd like to get there in daylight."

He had a point, and Katie took her hand from his.

He pulled forward, whistling a familiar Christmas tune, *Oh, Christmas Tree*. He told her it reminded him of his Katie tree. He'd probably wear it out in early May. Roker razzed him about it, but it was all about love, so Jeff laughed and ignored Roker. The man was single. What did he know?

Katie thought Jess up on High Road might have an opinion on that. She still had a question about Kevie, though.

"Jeff, what do you think Kevie had that he couldn't put in a car with someone else?"

"There's no telling. Remember those clams we dug up when we were kids? We carried them to town from out at your grandmother's. I don't think anyone would have let us inside their car." He chuckled. "It didn't help that we were covered with mud."

"A ride would have been nice, though. How did we carry them? Wasn't it in the Lil' Dude?" The Dude was Katie's twelve-foot sailing skiff. That summer Jeff, Katie, and all their friends had sailed around the islands in it. It seemed there wasn't a day they weren't out on the water.

"Ha!" Jeff laughed. "I do remember that. We had so many clams we nearly capsized. Twice. We finally made Bennie and Bobby get out and swim. Do you remember? We towed them with a rope."

"And their feet and hands were blue by the time we pulled them out of the water at the town float." Katie was laughing, too, and she wished she wasn't. It wasn't doing her stomach any favors.

"Don't you think a few people saw us in that boat

and felt sorry for us? Oh, those poor kids. Why doesn't one of those lobstermen stop and help them out?" Jeff's eyes twinkled. "We'd have refused if they did. Wouldn't we?"

"I get it. Kevie's doing fine, even though I'm freezing, even in here. I still want to know what he was carrying."

"If people had checked on the Dude that summer, they'd have regretted it. Sometimes it's best not to know."

"Then, let's change the subject. What's at the Point? It'll be dark when we get there." And cold. Katie wanted her fire, well, Jeff's fire, built with his hands, and her warming in front of it on the sofa. She wanted him, next to her in bed, the heat of his skin against hers. The Point? That was for summer and sunshine and languid starry nights, even if Maine evenings did require a blanket in the middle of July.

"What do you want more than anything in this world?" Jeff downshifted as the grade of the road increased. That meant they were coming up to the hawk's nest. This time of the year it would be unoccupied.

Katie considered Jeff's question as she looked at the empty nest high in the trees. At Christmas, it had been a snowy mound. Jeff told her a number of years back, an old bird had wintered over three years in a row. Then it was gone, and the nest had once again become a summer residence, just like most of the waterfront homes across the island. Now, with the sun of the past week, it showed bare woven sticks teetering at the top of a tree, a fantastic display of the birds' ingenuity, but lifeless, nonetheless.

Once she would have answered Jeff's question with, "My grandmother's house," and she wouldn't have had to think about it. Now, Nina's words haunted her. The style of the house doesn't matter. Only the love that fills it is important. Carver House, rebuilt and new again? It wouldn't give Katie her grandmother back, or Nikki's gift of a ring, lost with everything else in the fire that took it all. The pies and the nights in front of her grandmother's old Franklin stove, they were in Katie's head, but they could never fill a new house, even if it was exactly the same. Smiling, Katie made her decision.

"You." She laid her arm atop Jeff's, and she rubbed the skin just where his thumb crooked against his palm.

"Me, what?" He chuckled. He pushed in the clutch, and pulling his hand free, he changed the gears once more, taking her hand in his when he was finished.

"I choose you. You asked, what do I want more than anything else in the world, and I choose you."

"Okay, you scamp. After me. What do you choose after me?" He sounded pleased, but he laughed it off. "Be serious about this. It's important."

"I am being serious. If I can't have you—"

"Not so fast, Dame Carver. I didn't say that. I said after me. You're not being serious, yet. I want adult serious." He slowed for Round Pond. It held the town water supply. A sign said No Swimming or Boating Allowed. After crossing over the small earthen dam holding back the water, Jeff speeded up again.

"Adult serious, Girl Scout's honor." Katie held up three fingers. "I choose Jeffie." She patted her stomach. There was just enough of a baby that she could feel the difference.

"Pregnant women." Jeff said it with dismay, but his face showed his amusement. "We'll be there in ten minutes. What do you want?"

"Winnie here." Jeff's question was bringing up all sorts of emotions, and Katie knew it must be the baby. This wasn't like her at all. Yet, she missed her friend immensely, and her eyes burned. She wiped at them carefully, hoping Jeff wasn't watching.

"Oh, honey, I know you miss her." He took her hand and kissed the back of it. "No tears allowed. I'll have to kiss them all away, and I'll have a wreck if I do." The cutoff from the main road was coming up, and he slowed to turn, releasing her hand once again to shift a series of gears to make the corner.

This part of the road was dirt and gravel all the way to the house. Katie knew the going would be slow, and Jeff's hands would be busy, especially when navigating past Lookout Ledge, the highest point on the island. It came at the end of a sharp incline, then the road immediately twisted and climbed twice as steeply.

She smiled at Jeff's words, and she did feel better. Hormonal pregnant women! And she was one of them! Jeff's hands worked the gears, and he turned the wheel to avoid rocks and depressions in the road. He was so busy, and as he hummed his little tune, he occasionally laughed, calling out, "That one's gotta be fixed before long." Then he steered around whatever obstacle was in his way.

This was real life, Katie decided. This ride to the Point was life boiled down to its bare essence. You held hands when you could, released them for a moment when you had to change gears, and when the road got really rough, sometimes you were doing completely different things, one person navigating the treacherous terrain, and the other person watching it all happen. It wasn't like all the sugary sentiments that said, "Love is both people having their hands on the wheel at the same time," or, "Love is like kindergarten: Never let go of the other person's hand."

No, if you held on all the time, you caused a crash. Two people couldn't continually be in control. Sometimes you had to let go and let trust come into the picture. Sure, ask for directions, or change out drivers when the trip was tiring, and when possible, hold hands as you traveled down the road. If you held on too tightly, people suffocated. Jeeps wrecked. Friendships faltered. Katie thought of Carver House's old Franklin stove, lost with everything else in that long-ago fire. It had metal doors to close up the firebox, containing the flames and restricting the air to make it burn brighter and hotter, so that you got the most heat possible out of the wood. A relationship was like that. Marriage, especially. Your vows were the doors. You closed up the firebox, and love burned ever hotter. Close it up all the way, and you choked the fire. A flame needed air, or it would smolder and eventually die. Just like Jeff driving with Katie at his side, there were always careful adjustments to make. Work at it long enough, and the adjustments became as natural as living and breathing. Refuse to make them, though, and you had no relationship. All you had was control.

She had discovered she had no control over the Point half a lifetime ago. The fire had taken all that away. Now it was like the hawk's nest. It was the living each day to its fullest that filled it up. She'd once wanted her grandmother's house back more than anything, and then Nikki had offered it to her. Yet, it was Jeff's house, now hers and Jeff's, on Moffat Cove that had become her home. Carver Point was the memory of her grandmother and the good times Katie had enjoyed while growing up there with all her friends.

Jeff slowed to spiral past Lookout Ledge, and with the engine growling in protest, he nudged her with his elbow. "So, have you decided, yet?"

"I may be stubborn, but I'm not stupid." She laughed her comment off. "Your question is about the Point, or else we wouldn't be out here. So, I'll bite. To be able to rebuild Grandmamma's house. Since that's impossible, now we can move on."

"Oh, no, we can't." He glanced at her, fighting a smile.

"We have the report, Jeff. You know where that leaves us. Nina on the ferry said to call up an architect and come up with an all-new plan, but I need to see where Nikki stands first. It is her money." Katie gritted her teeth. The pull up the steep incline was doing a number on her. It seemed the baby didn't like going uphill.

"I get it. Everything hinges on your cousin, right?" Before he could continue, he topped the rise and cut left to follow the road, immediately hitting his brakes and coming to a full stop. A large branch lay across the road.

"That's the last straw, Jeff. Don't move." Katie began to fumble her seatbelt off.

"The last straw? You're the one who said it, but I guess you're right. She really does have all the money." He looked straight ahead, one hand on the steering wheel, and the other on the gear lever, his eyes evaluating the blockage.

"I don't care about money. Baby says move." With that, she threw the door open, and leaned outside for the second time in one day. She barely had the wither all to think, and her mouth was occupied, but if she could have barked out her feelings, she knew what she would say. Jeff, you did this to me. Why can't you be the one to lose your stomach twice in one day?

She wouldn't mean it, of course. It was the thinking it that make the moment almost acceptable. A baby in winter. On an island. With gravel roads. What had she been thinking?

Of course, that was the entire problem. She hadn't been thinking, or this wouldn't be happening.

"Katie, are you all right?" Jeff touched her on the arm, holding out the box of tissues from the console.

"In a minute." She spat and sat up, taking the tissues, and looking straight ahead. At least she felt better with her stomach emptied. Maybe the chili hadn't been a good idea. "Whatever you're showing me, it had better be good."

"It will be. Trust me. I'll be right back after I get the road cleared."

Katie watched him dragging the branch out of the way, the ends of his unmanageable hair loose under his knit cap, and his strong legs barely contained in his jeans. She did love that man, and he'd better be glad for it. If she didn't, the next six months wouldn't be worth it. Losing your stomach on a daily basis? Baby Jeffie, she thought, you'd better be beautiful, because you might be the last of your line.

By the time Jeff returned, she was over her moment of self-imposed pity, and she was able to smile. It helped that he looked perfectly contrite, as if he wished he hadn't forced her to come. Good, she thought. I feel exactly the same. They were almost there, though, so she would see what they'd come to see. After all, the ride home from here was only a couple thousand feet shorter than the ride from the Point. This, she could do. For Jeff, this she could do.

It was Jeff picking up her hand and giving it a kiss that really salved her spirit. Her preacher man Jeff, always coming to her rescue. In spite of this baby testing her limits, she loved Jeff, and if the Point fell off the island, she would still live out the happiest existence anyone had ever known.

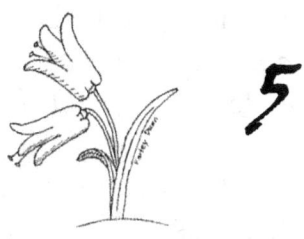

5

"What is that, Jeff?" Katie frowned. The question was rhetorical, because it was unmistakable. It was an aluminum-sided trailer house. Still, Carver Point was private property, and that trailer shouldn't be on Carver land.

"What?" He parked the Jeep across the grassy expanse that fronted the wood gate leading into the yard proper, looking very smug.

"Stop it. Someone's squatting on our property. It's against the law." Katie pushed against his arm. She remembered what he had told her the summer before. For the fourteen years she'd been away, he'd come out and checked on the property regularly to prevent this very thing from happening.

That was when she realized this was exactly the reason he'd insisted they come out today. He'd heard about this, and he knew she'd want to know. He was right. She certainly did.

"I see a sign on the side. I think it has a phone number. Where's paper and a pen? I intend to get that number down and call someone to get this removed." She was already digging in the glove box as she fumed. That episode with her stomach back on the road? Fiddlesticks. It meant nothing to her against this.

"Do you want your gloves?" Jeff held them out to her.

"Thank you. Hold this." She took the gloves with one hand and slapped a small pad and a clicker ballpoint pen onto his palm. She tugged the gloves on, and she glared out the window. "Just because there's no house here, and it's winter, they think they can move in, and no one's going to notice. A decade ago they might have gotten away with that—"

"No, they wouldn't." Jeff still wore his smug expression.

"Right. But if you hadn't been here, they might've. Well, I'm back, or haven't people noticed that?" She had her coat buttoned, and she tugged a knit cap over her head, preparing for the wind. It was nearly always windy at the Point. That's what a point of land on an island meant: exposed, and therefore, windy.

"Oh, I think they've noticed." Jeff nodded his head and looked out his window. There was nothing for him to see, except a wall of greenery. The real views were past the wood gate, where the ever-prevalent spruce and its accompanying undergrowth were cleared. His face, reflected in the glass, grinned.

"You sit right here, and then we've got some phone calls to make." Katie pointed a finger at him, and realizing how condescending that appeared, she made her hand into a loose fist. "Sorry, Jeff."

"No offense taken. Go. Get your numbers. We'll get this all sorted out." He held the paper and pen out to her. "Don't forget this."

"Thank you." She took it and pulled the door handle, releasing the door and stepping outside. "It's cold out here. And to think, when Grandmamma's house was built, people lived here year round. Crazy."

"Crazy." Jeff chuckled.

Katie marched over, her feet walking across last summer's grass, and she clicked the pen out, ready to scribble down the number and get back into the car. Only after she pressed the pen to the pad ten times, writing all ten numbers—as well as scribbling in one corner when the ink wouldn't come out—did she notice the words above the number. Chetwynde Architectural Design and Construction. To the side, it added in a cursive script, Almon Chetwynde, Owner.

She turned to look at Jeff, to see him waving cheerily through the window. Slipping her pad into her breast pocket and forcing her hands into pockets of their own, she headed towards the car, not exactly happy.

"You knew what this was." She pulled herself inside and closed the door hard after her. "So explain it."

Her concern had to do with the engineer's report, the fact—and it was a very real fact—that the original house couldn't be restored, and it was only that exact house her cousin had agreed to fund. Not a post-and-beam glass-infused structure, or a low-slung cottage, but an 1892 manse filled with porches and family history. They couldn't do this on their own.

"It's simple. I'll tell you about it on the way in. I want back on a paved road by dark." Into town, he meant. On the island, everything was either in—towards town—or out—any other place on Rockhaven. His comment about the dark was obvious, too. Past the end of the driveway, the dirt and gravel road was easily navigable in the light. At night? The potholes and frost-heaved rocks all looked the same. He shifted into gear and turned the vehicle around.

"Chetwynde." Katie pulled the pad out and looked at the name. "Didn't we know a Chetwynde growing up?"

"You're making the connection. John. His dad's Almon." Jeff smiled. "John lived up on the Reach. They were summer people like you, but he spent his summers at camps off island. Tennis, usually."

"His father's an architect. Hmm."

"No, John's the architect. His dad has the money."

"And you invited him to do what?" That worried Katie, and especially that Jeff would do it without consulting her first.

"You need the rest of the story. John's firm is finishing up a new build out on Smalley's Point." It was an isolated area overlooking Rockhaven's sister island, East Haven. "I met him in town, and he'd heard the old place on the Point might be going back up. He has another project coming together, a remodel in town, and he'd be interested in bidding on ours. He could cut out some of the costs, since his crews would already be on site."

"They'll be on the island, anyway. The Point isn't a building site, yet." Katie took a deep breath, holding on as Jeff navigated the turn to head back towards Lookout Ledge. At least the baby didn't seem to mind going downhill as much as he had uphill. "I think he doesn't want to move the trailer out until winter's over, and parking at Carver Point is convenient storage."

"Maybe, but he said he'll be glad to look at the reports and evaluate it, maybe even come up with some tentative options. All I need to do is shoot him some parameters so he'll know what we need."

Katie thought on that. If they had something on paper, then when they talked to Nikki, she'd have concrete examples to weigh over in her mind. That might be a very good thing.

"Okay, Jeff. You keep track of this—" She put the pad with the number on the console. "—and I'll think over what I'd like out there. It has to respect the house my grandmother lived in all her life."

"Of course." He took her hand and squeezed it, then released it to downshift to navigate a pothole.

"And a downstairs bathroom. Grandmamma hated having to climb the stairs every time she had to go."

"Downstairs. Got it." He smiled.

"A garage. Do you want a garage?"

"A garage would be nice." He chuckled. "Any porches?"

"Oh, Jeff. Porches everywhere! That was my favorite thing about Carver House. It had porches everywhere, with a porch swing. I would love to have a porch swing."

"Write it down." He picked up the pad and held it in the air. "Porch swing, number one priority. We can't leave that out."

Katie laughed, taking the pad and putting it back on the console. "Will he charge us for this?"

"Oh, I'm certain, if we decide to build. He did say he'd offer us a good deal, though."

"It's just that it's not our money we're spending. Maybe we should leave off the garage. One porch, maybe. Surely Nikki wouldn't mind paying for that." She smiled as she said it, but it wasn't what she really wanted.

"That's not what John said. We're to shoot him ideas. Let your cousin knock them down." He pulled onto the main road. His headlights were on, and with the tarmac, he picked up speed.

"It's getting my hopes up that worries me." She'd lost everything a long time ago, and it had been hard. But she'd done it, forging ahead to a new life in Boston. To have it offered back to her stirred up longings that she didn't want to have to squelch once again.

"You let me worry about that. Oh, I bet you don't know something else." His face lighted up in an impish grin. He held her hand full time by then.

Katie laughed. "Apparently not, or you wouldn't be saying that."

"The remodel on Ritchey's store is John's other

project. How about that?"

"Good for John." Katie nodded, finding it oddly satisfying. The old pack was coming back together, all connected in one way or another, with a new man or two to fill in the gaps. Who else would she see before her first year as an adult in Rockhaven was over? Apple Dumpling? Babes Baker? Maybe even Bennie and Bobby Reynolds? How great would that be, to have everyone together once again on Rockhaven Island?

She put that aside, though. She had to get the house completed first. Otherwise, where would everyone stay?

6

"Janine! Al! I'm glad you could make it this morning."

Katie was in the church foyer, welcoming Jeff's flock to the Sunday morning services. It was rare for Janine and Al to miss, although it was almost equally rare for them to be on time. With four boys, who could blame them? Janine had once confided to Katie that it was sometimes the only hour of the week she got with just Al. Someone else got to enjoy her boys for a while. Janine had chuckled as she'd stressed the word enjoy.

"Kevie, the man with a plan!" Katie raised her fist and gave him a fist bump. He grinned and returned it. The youngest two, Karlton and Keithie, were in an on-going tussle as they came through the door. Janine groaned and told them in a tightly-controlled voice to find their Sunday school room now. Konnar didn't come in at all, but as the door closed, Katie could see him standing just outside.

"He wanted to ride up front." Al laughed, like it was no big deal. "Keithie got the honor. It was a bit of divide and conquer. It worked until we got out of the truck." He snapped his fingers at the two youngest, still arguing, calling out, "Now, boys. Off to your rooms."

"I'll check on him." Katie smiled. She was learning to enjoy being the minister's wife, because it gave her an open door to step into all sorts of problematic situations. People let her attempt to resolve issues that other islanders wouldn't be allowed near.

"Thank you. Janine knew you'd be glad to talk to him. She's already inside, so I'm heading in. Send someone for me if you have any problems." He looked relieved and disappeared into the auditorium, where the adult class was about to begin.

Jeff was involved in welcoming Archie Coombs to the service. It was his second visit, and Katie was convinced her pleasantries his first time with them was the reason for his return. Jeff held one of the man's hands in both of his, and he laughed at something Archie said. Katie touched her husband on the elbow and said, "Door." He nodded to her, and she stepped outside.

"Konnar, it's cold this morning." Especially as Katie didn't have her coat on. It was on the rack, and she hadn't thought before deciding to do this.

"I'm mad." As if that told the entire story, and even perhaps that Katie was intruding on his private misery.

"One of those days. I have them sometimes." Katie shivered, but at least she had long sleeves. If it were windy, she wouldn't have made it this long. "Sometimes telling someone helps."

"I called front. I called it, and it was mine. Then Dad made Keithie sit there." He wiped at one eye with his hand.

"Did he say why?" Al had explained to her, but had he told the boys? Or maybe it was like telling them to go to their Sunday school classes. He got tired of their behavior, so he told them to just do it.

"Yeah. The little twerpies were fighting again." He coughed—the cold, probably—and he stuffed both his hands in his jacket pockets. "I don't like little brothers."

"Did it work?"

"Did what work?" He looked at her. That was progress.

"Did your brothers stop fighting?" She smiled at him encouragingly. Maybe he would smile back.

"Until we got· here." He almost grinned. "I hit Keithie on the knee all the way to church."

"And he didn't say anything?" Katie smiled, this time because it was funny. Paybacks, the boys would probably call it.

"I would've hit him harder." Konnar snickered, as if it were a good joke. "I'm cold. Can we go in, now?"

"Absolutely. I'm cold, too." Katie pulled the door open and followed him inside. He heaved his coat off, tossed it to land underneath the others on the rack, and tore off to his classroom. Jeff was already in the auditorium, moving among the pews to greet people she had welcomed, but who had bypassed him. He was good at that, searching out people, and making them feel as if they were the most important people on the island. It was why crowds showed up even in the worst of weather. It was because they felt like Jeff really cared.

On the right she found Roker. She smiled at who was next to him. Since Thanksgiving, Roker and Jess from up on High Road had become a common sight together across Rockhaven. Katie searched, hoping to see Neil Foote. He didn't often get out in the coldest of weather, and she wasn't overly surprised not to find him.

It was more surprising not to see Babbitt George. Katie had seen Brookie and Mara, his children, come in early. And Libby, Babbitt's wife, was on the second row. Shrugging, Katie let her eyes move on. There were a dozen places he could be, from the usher's box to filling in for a Sunday school teacher who hadn't made it in. She smiled at the Schutmaats. They were the most faithful in the entire congregation. It helped that they lived on 4th Street, just blocks from the church. Ada Simpers had made it in, in spite of living the other side of town. And Bryan Nickerson, one of Jeff's eager beavers, those trusted church members that always went overboard to see that they were involved in every activity, no matter how much it got on other people's nerves. Katie didn't mind. She liked eager beavers.

It was the Watson-Strykers that reminded her of Debsy, their daughter, in the Christmas pageant. The girl had abandoned her part to take off for the rest-room, leaving Katie to assume her role. And the girl had been the adorable star of the production, carrying the final Christmas star to hold it over the baby Jesus. What spoke well of the Rockhaven Town Church flock was that the congregation found the child charming in spite of it, and that had endeared them to Katie.

Katie hadn't seen them since Christmas, and she made her way to Kayline, Debsy's mother. She touched her on the shoulder to get her attention.

"Katie! Good morning!" Kayline set her Bible and gloves to the side and stood, grabbing Katie in a quick hug. "I'm so sorry we haven't made it to services the past few weeks. Jerry's father, and then Little J took the flu. We can't seem to get ahead for falling behind." She laughed. "Are you doing okay, with the baby, I mean?"

"Most days. When I remember not to ride the fer-ry. It's good to see you here today." Katie made to move on, only to have Kayline grab her wrist.

"If you've just a minute, I have something for you."

"Of course." Katie had no idea what it could be, and she'd only meant to connect with the family, not intrude into their morning. However, Kayline was already opening her Bible, and she pulled out a folded sheet of tablet paper, the sort pulled from a wire bind-ing.

"This is from Debsy, and she's only three, so take

that into account. She really wanted you to have this." She pressed the paper into Katie's hand. "Jerry and I, well, we want you to know how much we appreciate you stepping in as minister's wife here. You are so good with our little ones. Thank you." She took Katie's hand in hers and squeezed it.

After a brief smile, Kayline sat, cutting off the conversation, but Katie was pretty sure that was because of the impending tears she'd seen. Now she felt bad about being irritated at Debsy during the play. She was three, and three-year-olds did three-year-old things. Katie guessed she would understand some day. Maybe this was her first lesson.

The organ started up as the signal for people to finish their visitation and move to their seats. After two or three more handshakes, and two whispered good mornings, Katie settled into her seat. She opened the folded paper, and on it, in bright and erratic crayon, was a sunflower, a sun, and a big red heart. At the bottom was Debsy's name, painstakingly written, although with a backwards "b."

Katie felt her eyes water, and there was a knot in her throat. What a sweet thing for the child to do, and she had clearly put a great deal of effort into it. The oversized heart got Katie to thinking, even as she pulled out her tablet to take notes on the morning service. Valentine's Day was only a month away. She would have to plan something special for all the children. Especially Kevie. He was turning twelve in March, but he wasn't too old for a little valentine fun.

Katie clicked her tablet on. Not all churches would

approve of their members—especially the minister's wife—having their personal devices out during services, but even before Katie had come to live full time on the island, Jeff had been very proactive in embracing the future. The building was set up with a Wi-Fi system everyone could connect to, and using online Bibles was encouraged. The congregation's favorite was one that allowed them to insert comments about certain verses, and the other church members could view them on their own devices. Once a month, Jeff coordinated the comments and published them in the church's weekly email. Katie's job was to provide a weekly email of the entire service for those who were stuck at home for the morning, and of course it went to all the summer people who attended, if they'd provided their email address to the church.

Katie had a few more people she'd put on her list. Winnie Catron, her best friend. Ritchey Hickox, Jeff's closest boyhood friend. Recently she had added Austie William's name to her list.

She was still searching for Babes and Apple. They had to be out there somewhere, and email? Surely everyone had email. It was the 21st century, after all. Then there were the Reynolds twins. Where were they hiding? It was as if they'd fallen off the ends of the earth. People can't just disappear. They have to be somewhere.

She would find them. Just give her time. The old gang would get back together one way or another. Katie had mentioned them in her private prayers enough, and she was convinced of one thing. God always came through, and she had no doubts this time. After all, she was back on Rockhaven, married to the childhood sweetheart of her dreams. If that wasn't the hand of God, what was?

God could do anything. This? It was a piece of cake. With God, everything was a piece of cake. Katie smiled at that. She also knew you had to wait for the cake to come out of the oven to enjoy it. Jeff? He'd baked for fourteen years. Now, God, Katie mentally sent up as she typed in the title for the morning's notes. Turn up the heat. It's time for the latest cake to come out of the oven.

Then, she set her tablet aside and stood for the first song of the morning. She began to sing, "How great thou art . . ."

She meant it, too, every single word that came out of her mouth.

7

"Jeff, I was finally able to reach Connie. She got back with me, thank goodness, and she said she'd see what the company could put together. She sounded hopeful." It was about going back to work, although it had to be something she could do from home. Traveling to Boston for employment was not an option.

Katie held a cup of steaming cocoa in her hands, and she looked out the broad expanse of windows that gave the living room a sweeping view of Moffat Cove. It was beautiful, even if the warmth of the past few days had melted the snows, leaving the winter-browned grass in sharp contrast to the vivid green of the surrounding spruce trees.

However, there was one particular part of the scene that wasn't beautiful at all.

"Sweetheart, that's not the solution." Jeff came up

behind her and wrapped his arms around her. He pulled her hair back and kissed her on the neck. "The island takes care of its own. See?" He pointed out past the dock to his boat. Roker was bundled up, and he was working on the engine. They'd see him disappear for a few minutes, then he would reappear, occasionally scratch his head, and then vanish once more. He didn't look as if he were making all that much progress.

"The island doesn't make the car payment." That, and Jeff's four-wheel-drive, and now the medical bills involved with an upcoming baby. Even with insurance, their share had dropped Katie's jaw.

"Neither does my wife working a part-time job. We'll be okay. After all, we have the house. See? We're fine." He leaned in and began kissing her neck again.

The house had been from Jeff's father, a family legacy bequeathed to him in his will. Katie was certainly grateful for that. Still, she studied the boat, seeing Roker reappearing once more, fully aware the problem had deeper roots still. And if Cousin Nikki did rebuild Carver House, they would have to assume the increased taxes, but how could Katie say no to her cousin's offer? She'd never have another chance to see Carver Point reborn without her cousin's generosity.

"Look, Roker's waving. I think he wants you." Katie jabbed her husband in the ribs. "Enough, Jeff. You'll wear a hole in my skin. Go help him get your boat back on the water. You've got lobster out there waiting in your traps. You can't leave them to starve to

63

death."

"I don't think pulling pots compares to spending time with you, but I'm at your command. I go, and I'll do all I can to meet Roker's demands of me." Jeff chuckled and bowed to her, looping his hand in a circle.

"You're too silly. I've got a valentine activity to put together, so you get out there and leave me in peace. Just because I'm home all day doesn't mean I sit around and twiddle my thumbs."

"Of course not." He was putting on his coat. "I can't imagine you twiddling anyone's thumbs, ever. My boat repairman and I will need something to eat when we get wrapped up. Can you find enough time to twiddle that together?" His eyes twinkled.

"Go!" She held up her cup. It still steamed. "Remember the thermos on the table. It has more of this inside. Roker will worship you for bringing it out."

"He'll worship you, but then, I think he already does." He vanished into the kitchen and emerged with it in his hands. He had his gloves on, and he pulled a knit cap over his head, making sure his ears were covered.

"I love you, Jeff." Katie waggled her fingers at him.

"Eh?" He tapped one ear, showing her it was covered.

"I love you," she called louder.

"What's that?" He pulled the cap from over his ear. "Say that once more?" He was grinning by then, though.

"Oh, you. I should kick you." She laughed. "You could hear me the entire time."

"You can't blame me. I like hearing you say you love me. I love you, too, Katie." He twisted the door knob, and he stepped into the sun, the faint sound of *Oh, Christmas Tree* trailing after him.

Katie shivered, watching him walk across the yard and out on the dock. Sunshine in Maine didn't equate to warmth. This time of year, it provided light, but that was it. Still, it caught on Jeff, light and shadow, showing him for the lobsterman he was. Broad shoulders. Long legs. His clothes fitting and not fitting at the same time. It wasn't that they didn't fit, just that they weren't loose, and neither were they tight. Rather, they were loose when he relaxed a limb or a muscle, and tight when he stepped forward or bent to pick up something. It was the look of a lean, muscled man, one who worked for a living, not someone who simply thought for his life's work. There was a difference, and seeing Jeff there, moving in the sun, the sharp shadows in vivid contrast told her how lucky she was to have found him once again.

Taking a deep breath, she turned away from the window. She had to jump into her valentine thing, or she'd never get it planned. With less than two weeks to go, it had to be something simple. Taking out a paper pad and pencil, she titled the blank sheet Love Spectacular. Then Katie was hit with what she considered a brilliant idea. Her Love Spectacular needed to be all about the children. Have the parents make cards for their little ones, do cakes, cookies, and special presents

65

all around. Then bring them all together for a banquet, with streamers and red punch and more. Parents could dress in red and white, and they could be the waiters and waitresses. They could have a father-daughter, mother-son dance, and finish with a fun, kid-friendly movie. It would be a family night to end all family nights. And if the kids didn't know it was coming, that would be even better, a surprise to top any Valentine's Day they had ever had.

Now enthused, she began to make a list of the children at the church, and it occurred to her that every other child on the island could join them. And families without children? Yes, invite them, too. Katie felt giddy with excitement. Connie Rivera and ALDMass could wait, at least until after Valentine's. Katie was going to be very busy until then.

8

"Nina, I have a proposition for you." Katie was having lunch at Harbor View restaurant. She'd decided to call it lunch, in spite of it being well after two, but her late lunch was purposeful. She needed Nina to have some free time to talk.

"Certainly. Does it involve money?" Nina winked, just a barely visible movement of one eyelid, as she rolled her damp towel into a compact cylinder. She pulled up at Katie's table, taking an uneaten hush puppy from her plate and munching on it. "Kent does make good puppies. We should eat here sometime."

"They are good." Katie pushed a half-eaten one to the back edge of her plate, and she laughed. She was pretty sure it was Nina who could take credit for the hush puppies, but that was what made it funny.

Nina smiled at Katie's response. "You didn't eat

very many, so I have to ask. The morning sickness? Are you completely over it?" She wiped her hands on her cloth, destroying her perfect cylinder, and clumped it in front of her. She watched Katie expectantly.

"Except on the ferry, but you saw that." Katie warmed with embarrassment at the memory and shook her head. Having someone see that still bothered her. "Jeff's off-roader sets it going if he drives too fast, but otherwise, I'm okay. Okay enough to enjoy these." She broke off a fresh end of one of the puppies and popped it into her mouth, chewing with a smile.

"Good. That wasn't your proposition, though. So, what can I do for you?" Nina sat back and smiled.

"It's almost Valentine's, and I've been thinking. I have what I think is a really good idea, but I need your opinion on whether it's practical." Katie pulled out a sheet of paper and a pen. She unfolded it to reveal a series of squares with a heading in each one. She chuckled. "Look at this. It's called my Love Extrava-ganza." The word Spectacular was blacked out, and Extravaganza printed neatly above it.

"For you and Jeff? Maybe you'd better plan this at home." Nina's eyes sparkled, and she turned the paper to look at it. As she skimmed the sheet, she rested a finger on each heading before going on. When she finished, she looked up. "I gather this isn't just for you and Jeff."

"It's for the island's children." Katie's enthusiasm burst out. "After the Christmas play, I saw how the people loved little Debsy, even as she abandoned her part to head off to the restroom right in the middle of the crucial final scene. Rockhaven's young people are the best thing the island's got, and their parents love them. Immensely. We need to let them know in the most extreme way possible."

"How extreme?" Nina's eyebrows were raised, and she looked ready to pull Katie back inside reasonable bounds, if necessary.

Katie reached to touch one of the sections of the paper. "I want it to be all about the kids. Like a surprise. It'll be like a Valentine's party at school, except the parents will give the cards. I've listed some of the children from the church, but I don't know everyone who winters over." She moved her finger to touch Little J's name, and the Peavey boys in their various blocks. There were Debsy, Brookie, Kern, Matt, and all the rest she'd been able to think of on the spur of the moment.

"And I'm to fill in the blanks?" Nina had begun to smile.

"For a start. I'd like parents to come in red and white, serving and entertaining the children."

"I'm following you. It's a kids' night out, one all about them." Nina had moved on to pursing her lips, like she was thinking.

"Yes. Exactly. Everyone involved." Katie knew Nina was the one to come to. She was a get-'er-done type character, and she'd be able to see Katie's vision.

"We need to think bigger, though. Not everyone will show up just for this."

"It's for their children. Surely, Nina—"

"Islanders around here love their little tykes, but

it's winter, and they get tired of them. So, let's up the ante. Let's make it about the school. That way we can plan it, even tell the children, and they won't suspect a thing." Nina winked again, one conspirator to another, and she grinned impishly.

"You'll have to explain that to me." Katie had pictured something similar to a school party, with the parents acting as room mothers, but that was her imaginative limit of school connection.

"We'll do an auction, or a raffle. The money we bring in can be used to do something schoolish, maybe playground equipment or books for the library. Or both! I've got a quilt I made during a March blizzard that shut the entire island down for a week about a decade ago. I thought my daughter might like it, but she's in South Africa. She has yet to express an interest in the quilt. There's our first item in the pot."

"I see." Katie did, too. "The kiddos can sell the tickets, and when their parents bring them up for the drawing, we have a banquet planned."

"Girl!" Nina laughed. "You and I are on the same page one hundred percent. Now, Kent collects sports equipment and model cars. I'm pretty sure I can talk him out of one or two. We have to have something to appeal to the younger set."

"Snowshoes. Jeff has a pair he's never worn, and my good friend Winnie gets free makeup and clothes at her fashion shoots. She always tries to get me to take some. I can have her ship me a box."

"Now we're riding the train right out of the tunnel. Let me think, who do I know not on your list? There's

Lavern's daughter, Spice. She's thirteen, so she goes in this box. And Ken and Ellen Amiro have three you've probably never met. They live up on Black Seal Cove out the other side of Smalley's Point. They homeschool." Nina put in their names, Ken Jr, Lane, and Sadie, with Ken in one box, and Lane and Sadie together. Twins, Nina said when she saw Katie watching. She also said the family tended to live off the land, so don't expect much cash to come from them. However, Ken and Ellen would work like draft horses if they thought it would benefit their kids. They'd be a good family for selling tickets.

Katie saw it all coming together. This could be better than she'd imagined. There was one caveat. The extravaganza was two weeks away, and that meant all this had to happen quickly.

Very quickly.

Thinking about it made her dizzy, and it wasn't morning sickness making her head spin. The whole island? What had she been thinking? Maybe it was like her wedding night. She hadn't been thinking at all, and now look what she carried around with her. At least any babies that appeared at the extravaganza already had parents to take them home. Whew!

Nina assigned her the job of heading out to the Amiro's. Nina said she'd like to just call, but it was remote, and out that direction the Thanksgiving blizzard had taken the phone lines down. The Amiros hadn't had good service before, and now? They needed a face-to-face meeting, and Katie was just the one to do it.

About then the door slammed, and the two women looked up to see Archie Coombs removing his coat. Nina placed her hand on Katie's wrist, whispering, "See? Just when I have a moment, in comes a customer. Don't want Archie riled up. I'd better take care of him. I'll get back with you."

Katie watched Nina shift gears, calling out to Archie, and teasing him into laughing with her. What a wonderful woman to have for a friend, she thought. What a wonderful place this was to live. Now, she had to find Black Seal Cove. If she headed west, she thought, towards the Point, then cut right at Upper Island Road, it would take her past John Chetwynde's new build on Smalley's Point and on to the Amiro's. It wasn't in close sailing proximity to Carver Point, which make it unfamiliar to her. Still, she couldn't get very lost. She was on an island. Every road had to eventually wind back to town, didn't it? Katie laughed at that, imagining driving around and around the island, all the roads dropping off into the sea, and never finding her way back again. It would be like an adventure. How had she seen it written? Today was a good day to have herself a good day. With that in mind, she also felt today was a good day to learn a new part of the island. By the time she was Ada Simpers' age, she might know the better part of it. Maybe.

Katie waved to Nina as she exited the building. She pulled her coat tighter around her throat, and she patted baby, whispering, "I love you, Baby. Be good and stay warm." With a beep, she unlocked her car door and slipped inside. She set aside the troublesome thought that before little Jeffie showed up, they might very well lose Jeff's four-wheel-drive toy or her wonderful blue Bug. Yet, that wasn't happening today, and probably not tomorrow, and for that she was grateful. It was up to Connie now. If ALDMass would get on the ball, then everything would work out fine.

As she pulled out, the sun caught her eye, and she flipped the visor down. Two things fell in her lap. One was Winnie's postcard of Monhegan with her warm sentiments on the back, and the other was a folded paper Katie hadn't seen. It had a man's name and phone number on it, and in Jeff's writing it said, "Willing to offer $22K for Jeep. Will call back next week."

Katie pulled to the side of the road and stopped, looking at the words with dismay. She knew . . . Jeff had told her . . . but this made it real. Too real. God, she sent up in a silent prayer, you cannot let this happen. You have to work this out. Jeff gives everything to you. This one thing. You can work out this one thing and let him keep his car.

That done, she pulled out on the road, and an online devotional she'd read that morning popped into her head. It had compared God to a sunrise. At times He makes His presence known in a blaze of glory, but He knows that if all we do is watch Him in worshipful adoration, no one would farm the fields, put roofs over their children's heads, or reach out to the lost. So, He lets the colors of the sunrise fade so humanity can get on with the business of life. Yet, like the sun, even though the brilliance of His beauty has faded in our eyes, He is still shining over us, bringing us life every minute of the day.

It was the getting on with the business of life that had Katie thinking. Maybe that's what God expected her to do. God had blazed through her life in July, bringing her and Jeff together, and now He was standing back and watching, and it was His way of telling her, "Get busy, Katie. I love you, but this life is yours. You get to live it. I'm not through with all the sunrises I'll bring you, but this day? That's up to you. Don't let me down, girl."

Katie knew what that meant. She planned to be back on the phone to Connie, just as soon as she left the Amiro's. If God expected Katie to be the one to live her life, then that's what she'd do, and by that, she intended to do whatever it took so that Jeff could keep his car. $22K? Not on that man's life were they taking $22K for that big green off-road machine. It was Jeff's, and that's all there was to it.

It hit home with her that she also had her Love Extravaganza on the burner. She steeled her backbone. There were no two ways about it. She would have to handle both. She wasn't about to let God down, or Jeff, either.

Any good minister's wife would feel the same, she was sure, even if she didn't quite know how she would manage to get it done.

9

"Good morning, Jeff!" Katie wrapped her arms around her husband. She'd said nothing about the Jeep, but she now checked each morning to see that it was still in the drive. If it was muddy with winter's grime, so much the better. It meant no one was headed up to look at it that day.

"Katie, sweetheart." He pulled her down to sit in his lap. Putting his hands on either side of her face, he kissed her on the lips twice, then once on each cheek.

"Hey, what's that for?" She laughed. "You have coffee breath."

"You didn't mind coffee breath last night." He chuckled. "I thought it might put you in the mood. Is that how they say it, in the mood?"

"Not since 1954. I'm meeting John in an hour, and I believe you have Roker waiting on you in town. So, that means you need to let me up, and good-man-Roker gets to appreciate your coffee breath for a while."

"He won't care. I've got a jug made up for him. That's John Chetwynde, with the plans, right?" He let her go and reached for his cup, with a chuckle and a wink. "Did he promise a garage?"

"He promised something buildable, and that means Nikki will probably nix the whole thing. My hopes are not up."

"What about the Love Extravaganza? I understand you've been out to the Amiros. How was that?"

"Wonderful! Did you know they built their house from trees felled on their own property? Ken cut them himself with an ax, and he and Ellen hand-sawed the boards for the house. That's impressive."

"Don't know about that." Jeff downed the contents of his cup and set it in the sink. "Seems to me hauling lobsters twelve months a year's pretty impressive."

"Jealous?" Katie was loving this. Jeff? Feeling like he needed to compete?

"You do know Ken and I were on the football team together at university. He has a degree in environmental science." He looked at her, his arms crossed, and he leaned against the countertop. "He's quite brilliant. Turned down a job with the EPA to move back here."

"No." Katie had been surprised to find their place out on Black Seal Cove to be tidy, well-designed, and perfectly pleasant. She guessed, with hearing that they home-schooled their children and tried to live off the land, she'd assumed they were hippies. "So, he could work anywhere."

"That's right. He loves here, though. Ellen teaches university classes for that online school in Arizona. It's how they make ends meet. She has a Masters in, um, foreign language, Latin, or something like that."

"I am impressed." And she was. Brilliant people choosing to live in the woods because they wanted to, not because they had to.

"Just don't tell them I told you. They like the homespun version better. They're good people. I'd love to have them part of the church, but they do their own religious instruction. Who can argue with that?"

"They're on board for the extravaganza, and I'm glad you told me about them. Two thumbs up for their family. Oh, and I got your message about Winnie calling. She didn't pick up when I returned the call. Did she say what it was about?"

He shook his head. "No, just for you to call, and now, I've got to go. I'll be away the entire day. If the shop on the mainland needs to keep the boat overnight, Roker and I'll ride back on the ferry. I'll call if I need you to pick us up at the landing."

"One phone, ready to go!" Katie pulled it from her back pocket to hold it up to him.

"I'm so lucky to have you." He leaned in and kissed her on the neck before moving up to her face, and kissing her again on the lips. "It's cold out, and they're saying snow before the weekend. Don't stay out after dark if you can help it."

"You be careful on the water. I don't want any body parts frozen. I like you in one piece."

"Yes, ma'am, Dame Carver."

"Ragsdale, you silly man. Go!" she said, laughing.

"You're always Dame Carver to me." He pulled her up and kissed her once more, before releasing her to begin pulling on his heavy weather gear. On the boat, and with temperatures in the thirties? It would be very cold on the water today.

Then he was gone, heading down to the dock and onto the float. He waved once as he rowed out to his boat. Starting it up took three tries, and even Katie could hear the knock that had him worried. Fix it now, he'd said, before he had to really fix it later. He'd expressed that with a deep breath before and a deflating sigh afterwards. Then he'd laughed, but it wasn't a real laugh, not the fun sort.

Katie pulled her things together. She and John were meeting at Ritchey's new store in town. She'd found that exciting, to get to see on the other side of the brown paper, but he'd laughed, telling her they were still in the tear-apart stage. Don't expect anything impressive.

As she headed out the door, her phone began to ring. Digging it out of her pocket, she saw it was Winnie, and she smiled, tapping the answer icon to bring her up.

"Winnie! I've been trying to get back with you. What's going on, Honey?"

"Sweetie, thank goodness you're finally at your phone. I have the most awful news! Hold on a sec." She spoke to someone not on the line, calling to them to hold the lemon. Just plain water was all she wanted.

Birds could be heard in the background, and it faintly sounded like kids playing. Winnie laughed. "I'm sorry, Sweetie. There's so much stuff happening. I can barely keep up."

"I can tell. What's the awful news?"

"Oh, that. You know Francois, your cousin Nikki's little man?" She stopped as if waiting on Katie to answer.

"Yes, I know Francois." How many men named Francois did her friend think she knew?

"Oh, right. Francois called, and he doesn't communicate very well, unless you're there, because then he can point, but on the phone, I have no idea. Bourgeois, and merci, but the rest? I say, oui, oui, oui, and he keeps talking. Hôpital. Do you think he meant hospital? Katie, Sweetie, are you there?" She spoke to someone else again, whispering loudly, "Don't worry. I can drink it with lemon."

"Did he mention Nikki's name?" Her cousin hadn't seemed all that peppy when she'd left at Christmas, but Katie hadn't considered she might actually be ill, seriously ill.

"Sweetie, when Francois calls, it's always about Nikki. We're not an item, you know. Grow up!"

"Did he say what's wrong?" Katie tried to push aside a sinking feeling.

"Cassé la jambe. He said that four times. I would have said a dance step, but nope. Not in this case. Sweetie, I have to be on the runway in two, so I'll try you again later. Give a hug to Jeffie and baby Jeffie. Bye, now."

"Talk to you then, Honey." Katie pulled up her translation app, and she said, "French to English." When it showed her it was ready, she said, "Cassé la jambe."

Her phone spoke back to her, "Broken her leg."

"Oh, my word," Katie breathed out loud. Then her phone rang again. She answered, "Katie here."

"It's Jeff. We've been ashore, and we're heading out again. We have to run the boat to a shop in Bath. Guess who I just saw at the ferry landing?" His boat roared in the background, and Roker called out hello.

"Who, Jeff?" All she could think about was her poor cousin Nikki. How bad must it have been to put her in the hospital?

"Ritchey's headed out to the island. But you'll see him when you meet up with John. I'm about to lose signal. Love you, Katie. Bye!"

"Bye, Jeff." Yet, he was already gone, and she was slipping the phone in her back pocket as she spoke. Poor Nikki. Then she thought of John Chetwynde. If Nikki was ill, was there any point in going in to meet with him? She might as well call him and say the whole thing was off.

Still, she did want to see Ritchey's new store, and if Ritchey was here, then she wanted to meet up with him, too. Sorry, John, she thought. All your plans for nothing. Katie breathed deeply, realizing she had hoped, in spite of what she'd told Jeff. She simply hadn't been brave enough to admit it. Now that she saw it falling through? It hurt, all over again. It really, really hurt all over again.

10

"It's certainly beautiful. Who wouldn't want to live there?" Katie felt a rush of . . . not envy. Missed opportunity. John hadn't simply put together some ideas. He had an entire floorplan designed, with full exterior elevations. One was in color, with the ocean in the background.

"I overlaid the virtual mockup onto images of the Point. It looks stunning, doesn't it?" John sat on the opposite side of the rugged work table, and he occasionally leaned over and tapped the keyboard to change the image. "If I drag this, you can see it in full 360 degrees."

True enough, Katie watched the image rotate, and there was Carver Cove down the hill. She looked closer to the dock and laughed. "That's me with Jeff. How'd you do that?"

John spun the computer around and looked closely, and he grinned. "I'm just good. No, really—" He chuckled. "—Jeff uploaded some photos from an event out there last summer. This is a photomontage of all of them. The program is designed to edit out people when possible, but it missed you two. I can't say I'm sorry, because this is absolutely perfect. You and Jeff, at your new home on the Point. By the way, that's the most beautiful location on the island, and that's God's truth. I envy you."

Katie wondered if he'd feel the same way when he learned their money seemed to be drying up even as they sat there.

"I felt a separate building for the garage would maximize your views, so I kept that on the outside of the yard proper. See, here is where I intend to cut back into the hillside . . ."

John had the floor plans up, and he pointed to the building that would tuck just off where his trailer was now. Then he moved to the house, showing her wide porches under cantilevered overhangs. The upper floor was ringed with clerestory windows, with larger ones on the south and the west to maximize solar gain. At the very top was a third-floor glass-enclosed rotunda, with a sharply-canted roof. The rotunda was for the views. The big windows tucked under the overhangs? Free heat, he assured her, can extend the season by an easy three weeks on either side, and she and Jeff would appreciate that in Maine's cool summers. But then, he didn't have to tell her about that, did he? And he laughed.

Katie saw more in the plans he worked through, the bedrooms with massive windows, and open decks and covered porches for whatever weather the island threw at them. She saw a little boy or a little girl running around, jumping off the dock, and begging to sleep alone in the cabin by the shore; and at the same time begging, Mommy, please come with me and stay until I fall asleep.

"John," she interrupted, "This is exactly what I pictured. The funds are from my cousin, so I have to run everything through her. I want this, everything, but—" and she laughed, looking towards the door, wondering where Ritchey was. Her escape. Her chance to pretend these plans were nothing, and to remind herself she had all she wanted in Jeff and the baby and the life she had been given on Rockhaven.

"If you wish, there are several scaled down options we can consider. The garage, of course. That can go, and if you stay with three bedrooms, or even two, the rest of the home remains perfectly functional. It's the views you're there for, in any case. As long as we have the glass, you'll never feel closed in at any time." He smiled, shifting the scene to a smaller floorplan of the house. "I don't have the exterior on this one, but imagine a smaller version of the one I showed you."

"If you can email me both—" Rapping on the glass door startled Katie, and she turned to see it opening, the knob held by a black-gloved hand.

"Hey, in here. I see cars out front." It was indeed Ritchey, bundled up and in a black overcoat. His head was bare, and his ears were red with the cold. "Katie,

John." He called with a wave, as he worked the coat off.

"Ritchey!" Katie stood and went to him. "Jeff can't be here—"

"I saw him in town. Look at you, pregnant mom! Give me a hug, you beautiful mother-to-be!"

"You fool! You think without Jeff around, you can get away with whatever you want. Well, don't forget. We have a chaperone." Katie laughed and let him hug her.

"John." Ritchey leaned across the table and shook his hand. "So, did you two decide on a house?"

Katie laughed. "John decided, and I fell in love. Now we have to get approval."

"From the town?" Ritchey frowned. "I can't see John's designs not passing muster. He's the best."

John chuckled. "Thank you, Ritchey. Keep saying that, because we're still disassembling this building, and you'll not see anything resembling progress today. No, Katie needs to get with her cousin, who is part of the entire process. We'll move on when that's settled."

"Good. Katie? Come tour my new store. I don't know that this one will make me rich, but it gives me a good excuse to come back home from time to time, and my wife can't complain. And because it's business, she doesn't feel obligated to tag along."

"Did you get to visit with Jeff?" Ritchey had her arm in his, and John walked at their side. "He'd hate not spending time with you if you can't stay long."

"Just a shake and a greet. The ferry was loading, and my car was next to go on. He made me promise to stay one night. I'll have to explain that to my wife, though." He grinned impishly.

"Well, I'm glad you're here, even for one night. Jeff will be back this evening, and you two can do whatever you men do together when you've got free time. Now, tell me all about how this is progressing." The store, she meant, but that's where they were, so she knew he understood.

"The building is all John's, so that I don't know about. I've got a team back in Houston putting together a product line specific to the island." He stopped and smiled at her. "I could ask you to do something for me."

"Sure. I don't know how I can help, but if there's anything, I'm glad to pitch in."

"I grew up here, and I don't think things have changed that much. Still, it's been ten years. I need to know who might be interested in working in the store. More specifically, who'd be good at working in the store. Can you do that, come up with some prospective employees?"

"I can do that." Me, was Katie's first thought, but with a baby on the way, she knew working in a store wasn't realistic.

"One other thing. I've got construction insurance through my provider in Texas, but they don't provide long-term coverage in Maine. Can I get some recommendations?"

Katie smiled at that. Could she ever? ALDMass was affiliated with New England Home, residential and business insurers. She now had a foot in the door with Connie Rivera. If she could bring a new business prospect to Connie's table, how could they not let her back in?

"I just might. Are you familiar with ALDMass?"

"Insurance? It sounds local. I don't think I am."

"The biggest auto insurer in New England. My employer." She laughed. "Well, my employer before moving here, but I'm in contract negotiations to get my job reinstated, and we have a subsidiary that handles residential and business policies. If you're interested, I could get your information and approach them for a quote."

"Katie Ragsdale, you're a lifesaver. I would love to have you handle this. Here. My card. My secretary will have all the information you need." He pulled a card out of his wallet and handed it to her.

Ritchey began asking John about the upcoming changes to the building, and Katie followed along, enjoying the conversation. Ritchey's offer wasn't exactly a new home on the Point, but perhaps it meant saving the Jeep. She breathed, "Thank you, God," as she slipped the card in her pocket. God did care. He really, really cared, providing the answer to something very important at just the right time.

Check off one box, she thought. Only about a dozen to go. Yet, she couldn't help the sense of satisfaction that filled her in knowing that God was on her side.

11

"**J**eff, I've been thinking about Cousin Nikki. We have to get down to see her." Katie looked out the kitchen window. She and Jeff were having an early breakfast. Ritchey was still asleep in the guest room upstairs.

"I've been expecting you to say that." He munched into a slice of toast lathered with purple jelly. "The boat's out of circulation for at least a week. Now might be a good time."

The boat hadn't been good news. The engine needed a complete overhaul, which was not cheap by any measure. Yet, their choices were limited. Katie and Jeff had prayed about it and decided to let the Lord have control in the situation. Maybe there was a reason they had a week free. Jeff had taught on Blind Bartimaeus the previous Sunday, telling the congregation how it was Bartimaeus' lack of sight that allowed him to hear Jesus coming. Yet, it was his faith that allowed him to call to the Master, in spite of the crowds that tried to silence him.

Perhaps, Jeff had whispered to Katie as they lay in bed afterwards, the Lord was removing one thing so they could sense something else, perhaps His hand guiding them another direction. They had to trust that He knew best in their lives.

Katie had agreed, but she'd seen Ritchey's insurance opportunity as saving Jeff's Jeep. Now she suspected it might be what saved Jeff's boat and his livelihood. The Jeep haunted her. She had trusted God, and she no longer felt she was on firm ground.

"Ritchey's heading out early. We could follow him, spend that hour on the ferry catching up, and head to Boston afterwards. What do you say?" He was behind her, whispering in her ear, and she hadn't heard him approach.

"Winnie's on St. Simons Island in Georgia. She won't be there." It was an empty place Katie couldn't fill at the moment.

"Nikki will be. That's who we're going to see. Since you met with John yesterday, it'll be a good time to show her the plans for the Point. What do you say? We can take your car. It'll be like a mini-vacation." He kissed her on the side of the neck, moving up to her jawline in a series of small kisses.

"Stop that." Katie felt the tears building.

"Stop?" He chuckled. "Why would I want to do that?"

She turned and put her arms around him. "I'm sorry. I feel lost today. Yes, absolutely. Let's spend the day together, you and me, all the way to Boston. With Nikki in the hospital, we might stay at the apartment. Francois surely won't mind. We have to plan for Sunday if we're staying over."

"I already have." He kept his arms wrapped around her.

"Who?"

"Al stepped up when I asked him. Guest speaker. What do you think about that?" Jeff chuckled. "Never thought of Al as a minister, but he tells great stories. I suspect the story of Jesus will involve a lot of boats and lobster pots."

"Jeff, you are such a good man. Al is so fortunate to have you for a friend, and you, him."

"Good morning. I see what I'm missing out on." That was from Ritchey, and he was still in his flannel pajamas and an old pair of Katie's furry house slippers. His hair was on end, a wild tangle that showed its losing fight against the pillow. "Do I get a hug, too?"

"Good lands, man, check the mirror before you come downstairs." Jeff laughed. "Don't forget you've got a ferry to catch."

"Yeah." Ritchey yawned. "Ten-thirty, something like that. Is there anything for breakfast?"

"Toast is done. I can throw in a few eggs, if you want." Katie pushed away from Jeff, letting her hand rest on his chest for a moment before turning to the fridge.

"Sounds good. Snow's starting up. Did you two

89

see that?" Ritchey turned to the window, yawning again, with one arm in the air, and his hand in his hair, attempting to pull it flat.

"It's beautiful!" Katie hadn't noticed. It must have just begun. "I hope it's coming down while we're on the ferry. I would love to see that."

"I've had snow up to my chin. I'm thinking Boston sounds like a really good idea." Jeff had moved beside Ritchey, the both of them looking out over the cove.

"They're expecting snow there, too. I'm connecting at Logan, and I got an update about possible delays. I'm remembering why I like Texas so much." Ritchey looked at Jeff with a grin.

"Cause you're a wimp." Jeff hit him on the shoulder with the back of his hand. "Real men stick it out, turning into Mainers."

"Real men know when to turn tail and run." Ritchey pushed on Jeff's shoulder in repayment.

"Real men? Ha! Remember this?" Jeff threw one arm around Ritchey's neck and began to rub his knuckles back and forth across the man's scalp.

"Hey! Surprise attack! Katie, call him off!" Ritchey's arms were swinging, but Jeff had him.

"I'm preparing breakfast. Sorry!" She wasn't really, as the eggs were still in the carton, but to watch two men behaving like teenage boys? It was too good, and more importantly, it was separation from her money worries. A day off the island would be good for her and Jeff. Boston. Her cousin, and if she had time, maybe she could look up one of her old friends. Perhaps a visit to Montecristo for a chimichanga. It'd been six months since being home, and she missed it. The taste of a well-made chimichanga could very well improve her outlook on life for a good many months to come.

Ritchey pulled away from Jeff, his hair worse than ever. He tugged his pajama top back into place, and he pushed his hair away from his face, laughing. "You got me there, Jeff. I get it. I did that to you all the time growing up."

"I've missed you being around, Ritchey." Jeff was red-faced and grinning. He bent his hands backwards and cracked his knuckles. "Texas is a long way aways."

"Yeah. You know, we never get snow in Houston. I do miss this, just not as often as you might think. Weekends at our beach house in Galveston, even in February—" He chuckled. "There's a lot to be said for Texas in winter."

"I'm sure." Jeff didn't sound so certain.

"Anyway, I'm taking back a place here on the island, so we won't be strangers any longer." Ritchey smiled brightly, and he looked like he was waking up. "I'll pull some clothes on, and I'll be back for breakfast."

"Oh, right." Katie was still holding the carton of eggs and watching the two men. "Sorry. I got distracted. It'll be ready when you get down."

He gave a casual wave to show her it was nothing, and he grabbed Jeff around the neck and pulled him into the living room, saying something about getting supplies to the island, and good heavens, did it have to cost $200 to bring a load of building supplies across?

Katie was glad for Jeff, having Ritchey stop over for the night. She was gladder for herself. She was getting a vacation, to Boston! She'd never thought of Boston as vacationland. After all, it was Maine that claimed vacationland on their license plates, but where you lived was never a vacation. It was the getting away that made a place special. She remembered Nina's words. A special place doesn't have to be on a tropical beach. It just has to be away. Different. Special.

There was still the Love Extravaganza in the works, but Katie had people working on that. Island people were responsible and willing to step up to the plate. This weekend, Katie wasn't accepting any responsibility at all.

She intended to have fun.

12

Katie caught herself falling back into her Boston surroundings like she'd never left. Yet, it wasn't the same, either.

After leaving Ritchey at the airport on the mainland, she and Jeff had followed Route 1 to the Interstate, and sped along through light snow at 70 all the way to New Hampshire and beyond. Seeing the familiar Massachusetts welcome sign had filled her with a giddiness she hadn't expected. She felt she was in a different world. A different century, almost, with the traffic, overpasses, and business-filled side roads.

Everything she saw in Boston she felt she could touch as if no time had passed at all. It was more like visiting a museum than a hometown, though, a place where everything was on display, and it had little to do with her. She remembered summer and standing overlooking the town harbor on Rockhaven. A man on the ferry had been snapping photographs, memorizing the beauty of the town, and she'd known he'd always remember Rockhaven exactly that way when he pulled out his pictures. It wouldn't be the winter storms or the spring gales that he'd see. This was the same. She was catching a glimpse outside of time. The people here, they fought with snowstorms, and shoveled walks to exhaustion. They had to shop in crowded stores on the way home from work. Traffic probably drove them to despair. Yet, what Katie saw was the reminiscence of good times that she'd stored away in her memory book of snapshots, totally independent of the reality of the world.

She knew that, and still, Boston tugged at her heart.

"What are you thinking, beautiful?" Jeff reached to her and took her hand.

"Nothing much." She gave a quick laugh to show it was no big deal.

"Is that a glum face?"

"I'm letting the city soak in. Everything here triggers a memory. I grew up in this place." She chuckled at that. She'd grown up here, yes, but not really, either. She'd grown more on Rockhaven each summer, at least in her own thoughts. Each June, the nine months in Boston slipped away from her like shedding an old layer of dead skin. She'd come alive in Rockhaven, new and glorious. It was a kid thing, she supposed. Summer. Friends. Freedom. Still, it had felt very real to her, and that made it real.

"You're not wanting to come back?" Jeff squeezed her hand, and his voice smiled at her. She looked up, and his eyes twinkled.

"To visit. How about we attend Trinity Church tomorrow?"

"Trinity?" He laughed. "So I can return guilt ridden that our services aren't better?"

"No! So I can show you off to all my friends. If it weren't Saturday, I'd love to stop in at ALDMass and talk to Connie, but that's not possible."

"To show me off to her, too?" He released her hand to brush the backs of his fingers down her jawline. "Anyway, aren't you in job negotiations with her?"

"We're hashing it out." She hadn't mentioned Ritchey's offer, and Jeff hadn't asked her about it. That meant Ritchey was leaving it all to her. It was the businessman in him, she supposed. Once you delegate, it's hands off. Responsible employees pull their own weight, or they're not worth their pay and need to move on to somewhere else. Katie was determined to pull her own weight on this. She wasn't a moaner, and she had wanted to surprise Jeff when his Jeep didn't have to be sold. Now she hoped she could mark his boat off the list of debts to be paid. However, false hopes weren't better than no hopes. She would tell him when she knew for sure.

"Hospital sign." Jeff pointed. Mass General, Right Lane. He tapped the blinker wand and moved over. "Would you like to stop for food before we visit your cousin?"

Katie didn't get to answer. A horn blared somewhere, then from a distance came the thudding sound of metal on metal, loud, tearing, and silence followed for a moment. Then another thud happened, with the shattering sound of glass. On the turnoff just ahead, brake lights became a string of bright red dots, and Jeff hit his brakes to slow down. A car cut behind them just as he slowed, and it stood on its horn for a long moment.

"Hey," Jeff called, looking in the rearview mirror. "I can't go anywhere, dude."

"Be patient." Katie patted him on the arm. "They'll figure it out. I wonder what happened."

"Sounded pretty obvious." Jeff was checking his mirrors, looking for traffic. "Is there another way to get there?"

"It's best to wait. It'll be like this anywhere. Boston traffic." She laughed it off, but this part was bringing back memories, too. How many times had she scheduled her errands around Boston's overtaxed roadways? She never had to consider that on Rockhaven. There, if you wanted to go, go. There were never cars on the roads. The worst thing she might encounter was someone in her favorite parking spot, and then, she just moved over two or three places. "This I don't miss."

"What?" They were inching forward, and Jeff was very focused on the brake lights just in front.

"Boston traffic. I don't remember noticing it all that much before. Now?" She chuckled. "How do these people stand it?"

"So you're not wanting to come back." He smiled, then pressed the brakes hard, as the car in front of him came to a complete stop. "If they'd stop riding their brakes, I could tell when they're slowing down."

"Jeff, Jeff." Katie cautioned him, taking a deep breath, and she pressed against her abdomen. "Little Jeffie doesn't like that. Easy on the brakes."

"Tell these dudes." A siren started in the distance, quickly growing louder. He looked at Katie, and he shook his head. "I'm sorry. I shouldn't blame them. Are you going to be all right?"

"If you stay off the brakes."

"Done. It sounds as though this might be something serious." They began to move forward again, and he remarked, "Finally."

They were well off the main road by then, and they could see flashing lights. There were police cars, one fire truck, and an ambulance. Orange-marked cones directed the traffic into a separate lane, and officers stood with arms outstretched, motioning to motorists to give the First Responders plenty of room. When they got close enough, they could see a small car wedged underneath a city bus. Both ends of the small car were crumpled. A larger SUV was behind both of them with its front bumper pushed underneath. A ragdoll of a woman was being laid out on a stretcher.

"How terrible." Katie felt her heart go out. "That car is crushed. How could that have happened?"

"We heard two impacts. I bet the SUV hitting the car was the second crash. We need to remember that poor driver in our prayers. At least they're close to the hospital. If you have to be in a crash, here's the place for it." The traffic was clearing, and Jeff had his blinker on to turn. "There's the park. We're here."

Red Sox field. He would recognize that. It was a man thing, to navigate by the means of sports venues. Katie had been watching for familiar restaurants, like Little Lamb and Harvard Gardens. Jeff had asked about food. Her answer? Yes, yes, and yes.

Even so, that woman on the stretcher wasn't far from Katie's thoughts. She would hold her up in prayer, but she hadn't looked very alive. How easy it was to lose someone you loved. You said good bye in the morning, and they never came home for supper.

"Nikki," she prayed, "be safe and healthy. Good Lord above, keep your hand on my cousin."

"Amen," Jeff repeated.

"I love you, Jeff." Katie rubbed his forearm tenderly.

"And I love you, too, Katie. We're here." He triggered the blinker once more, and he pulled into the parking garage.

13

"Jeff, I hate this." They were in the elevator, thankfully alone, and she glanced at the bag he held. It was their laptop computer with John Chetwynde's house plans for the Point. She touched it with the end of her index finger. "This embarrasses me."

"Sweetheart, your cousin did offer, and we'll never know if we don't ask." He lifted her chin and kissed her on the lips, and he smiled. "Remember, all she can do is say no."

"She can laugh at us." It wasn't the asking about the house so much as doing it while Cousin Nikki was in the hospital. They should be here for no other reason than to support her emotionally. Bringing the plans in like this? It felt like they were opportunists, here to take advantage.

"Then let me walk in first. I can pull the computer

out, she can laugh at me, and when I collapse in mortification, you can come in and scold me for bringing the house up while your cousin is in her current situation."

That got a laugh from Katie. "I can't do that. It would be a lie, like we were dishonest."

"Then let's be honest, ask her if she feels well enough to look at a really good plan an architect has put together, and if she doesn't? We won't need to open the computer at all. Is that a plan?" He smiled brightly, like a teenager who had just presented an audacious adventure as something ordinary and practical.

Yet, when he put it that way, it sounded perfectly logical.

"Have I ever told you how lucky I am to have married you?" She tiptoed and kissed him on the cheek.

"Today, or in the past week?" He fought a grin as he asked it. "I don't mind hearing it again, as often as you want to say it."

"You!" She slapped him on the shoulder as the elevator reached their floor and dinged. The door disappeared into the walls, and the pale colors of the hospital corridor opened before them.

"My lady." Jeff motioned with one hand, like a servant from two centuries before.

"It's Dame Carver to you, buster." She laughed, stepping outside. "This is a beautiful building. All this glass. I guess I expected lots of concrete and florescent lighting."

There had been some of that, but not here. Even in the depths of an early February, sunshine flooded the space through walls that were more glass than solid substance.

"There. Reception. Hold on, Katie." Jeff stepped to ask the final directions to Nikki's room. He looked every part a Mainer out of his element in his heavy coat, his hair teased by a knit cap and much static electricity, and his wide lobsterman's shoulders.

That was what Katie loved about him. On Rockhaven he was in his element. Completely. Even in the church, he fit like a glass doorknob in a Victorian house. It works because it's the only way it can be. Here, with all the svelte and inner-city décor, and the people who matched it so well, she truly saw Boston as she never had before. Jeff fit the island, and the people on the island fit Jeff, because they were of a kind. Alike. Attuned to the same needs, wants, and desires. They loved island life, and in that love, they became the island. Then, Rockhaven loved them back.

It made her wonder how Ritchey saw Rockhaven after being gone so many years. Did he fall back into a comfortable pattern, or did it fit roughly on his shoulders, the place and the people lacking the polish he'd grown accustomed to in Houston?

Katie couldn't help but smile at that, picturing Ritchey in his flannels and her old house slippers, with his hair sticking up on end. When he and Jeff had stood next to each other at the window, they could have been brothers, for all the difference in them. Nah, she thought. You can take the boy off the island, but you can't remove the island from the boy. These polished city people had never been to Rockhaven, not to live. They didn't look like Rockhaven, because they'd never lived Rockhaven.

"Mademoiselle Katie?"

She turned to see Francois at her elbow. "Francois! Jeff, my husband, and I are here to see Nikki." She pointed to Jeff still at the desk, looking over a pamphlet with the attendant.

"Ah, Monsieur Jeffrey. This way. I take you." He touched Katie's elbow gently, giving an almost imperceptible bow of his upper body.

"Jeff, we have a guide," she called, waving when he looked up. "Francois's here."

"Francois!" Jeff waved back before turning to disengage from the attendant and walking their way.

"Monsieur. This way." Francois nodded to Jeff in the same half bow, more a slight movement of his head, really, and leading off down the corridor.

"Winnie was wrong." Katie whispered her announcement to Jeff. "Francois speaks very nice English. I didn't have any trouble understanding him, and his accent is very engaging."

Francois had stopped at a door, and he knocked before stepping partially through. He spoke in a quick and fluid French before turning back to Jeff and Katie with a smile, his head going down again, saying, "Monsieur, Mademoiselle, I take you. This way."

"Thank you, Francois." Katie paused to put her hand on his forearm and smile at him.

"Mademoiselle." He smiled back.

"I think you've maxed out his English," Jeff whispered to Katie as they entered the room. However, he also looked the man in the eyes and recited his thanks for his help.

Inside, Cousin Nikki was covered with a brown houndstooth comforter, and her hair was heaped high on her head, with a vibrant scarf tied around it for a flamboyant touch. She was finishing up a jab of brilliant lipstick and closing the case. Her hand shook as she searched for a place to put it and finally dropped it beside her onto the bed.

"Your things. You must put them there." Nikki pointed to a brown leather sofa stretched beneath a wall of windows flooding the room with light. Beside it was a cream recliner, also in leather. It held a man's overcoat draped across the back. She took several shallow breaths when finished, and she looked like she struggled.

"How are you, Nikki?" Katie stepped forward to give her a kiss. She leaned in, only to have Nikki grasp her hand in both of hers as she stood back up.

"Non, my little Katie. We talk about you. I am so glad you are here. I have something for you. Francois. Francois!" She covered her mouth and coughed, before pulling several tissues from a small box, and patting the corner of her mouth. "My apologies. Francois!"

Nikki's eyes were reddened, and Katie noticed how pale and frail she looked. It had been less than six months since her cousin had arrived at her Boston apartment. She had used a walker even then, and her balance hadn't been great, but she had exuded fire and energy. Now Katie was truly worried.

After a short exchange between the two in their

beautiful and flowing French, with Nikki's words roughened at the edges, and Francois in a tone barely more than a whisper, Francois pulled several file folders from a bedside drawer. He held them out, fanned, and Nikki looked in two before selecting one. Francois placed the others back in the drawer and nodded before exiting the room.

Jeff had taken one of Nikki's hands, squeezed it, and moved to the sofa, where he sat with his coat on the arm, and his elbow resting atop it. The laptop bag hunkered on the floor at his feet.

Nikki laid the folder on the bedding in front of her and opened it. She smoothed the top paper. It had an official look to it. "Pardon Francois. His English is only a few words. He is a good man, though. His father was my driver many years in the past. He is in Lyons. He no longer drives, and Francois is anxious to return to him. Il ne sera pas longtemps maintenant." Nikki sighed broadly, once again running her hand over the paper.

"What was that you just said, Nikki?" Her cousin still held one of Katie's hands, and her question caused her to release it.

"Ah, ah, the thoughts of an old woman. You do not see it, I am sure, but I am very old, my little Katie. Very old. Your American doctors agree with me, although those in France did not." She laughed brightly, but it was filled with more resignation than amusement. "I think they humored me."

"Will you tell me what you said?" Katie sat on the bed, and she placed her hand on Nikki's.

"A saying for a very old person who has received unwanted reports. I would mean the words to say, ah, it won't be long now." Nikki nodded as if she'd taken care of something she didn't really want to reveal, and she patted the corner of her mouth with the tissues once again.

"So, you're getting out, soon?"

"Katie." Jeff stepped up beside her. "I think I understand. Nikki, has the staff here given you bad news?"

"Ah, what is bad news to an old woman?" She smiled, waving his question away with her hand. "Bad news is an old friend that turns against you, or a storm that strands you without fine wine or good food. My news? It is what a woman of my age should expect."

"You will be well, though. You'll be okay." Katie felt Jeff's hand on her shoulder and reached for it, wrapping her fingers under his.

"Everything will be, as you say, okay. Now, though, this I wish to discuss." She patted the papers twice with a splayed hand. "I wish you to start my house now."

"Your house?" Katie felt herself floundering. It seemed all she could do was ask empty questions. Jeff squeezed her hand, and she tried to relax.

"Pardon, my dear. I will claim it for a time, but it will be yours. If we do not start now, I may never see the end. I do so want to see it as it stands completed. Look, this." She pushed the papers Katie's direction. "It is all signed and ready. I need you to look over this and see if you approve. Then sign, and we are ready to

105

go."

"Nikki, do you mind?" Jeff held out his hand, and he took the papers from her when she nodded. He flipped through the sheaf and frowned. "This is—" He paused and faced the windows, and flipped back a page, before turning to the women again. "Katie, your cousin is being very generous. This is an open line of credit for construction of the new house on the Point. I think you'll be able to keep your garage."

He handed Katie the paperwork, and she flipped through it, only to have Jeff stop her at one point to show her a figure. Katie dropped the papers to her lap to look at her cousin.

"Nikki . . ." Katie's eyes welled up, and she couldn't say anything else.

"Non, non. I have more than enough, and you, my little Katie, are my only living relation. How can I not gift this to you? For your little one I will do this. You will let me, oui?"

"Oh, Nikki. You are so sweet. The architect just emailed us sample designs for the Point. They're tentative, but they're something we can show you. They can't rebuild the exact house, so he wanted to try something completely new. He sent me two different plans. Would you like to see them?"

"Oui! I had so hoped, but I did not want to ask. It has been so busy for you, with the baby, I am sure, and I was afraid you would find it difficult to make the plans so quickly. Now, where are they?"

Jeff had the computer out, and he opened it and pulled the plans up. Nikki oohed, and she aahed, exclaiming the windows were pictures to be seen from the inside, and it reminded her of her chalet in St. Moritz. Oui, oui, she exclaimed over and over.

"You will stay at the apartment, oui?" Nikki made sure to ask that, telling Katie that Francois had a room at the Wyndham right beside the hospital. The apartment was empty for the foreseeable future, and she simply must use it if they were staying over.

Later, leaving the room, with Nikki pleased but wan, although noticeably hoarser, and a hospital aide settling her for an afternoon rest, Jeff located a staff member to find out more about what Nikki had meant when she said it wouldn't be long. They soon discovered there was ongoing complications from advanced osteoporosis and several medications Nikki had taken for years. They were unsure whether the hip would ever heal, and worse, her spine had been fractured in the fall. Because of the extreme weather, they were also fighting the possibility of pneumonia. She didn't have it at this time, but with her lack of mobility? It was a concern.

The news brought home the reality of what Katie's cousin was facing.

After a warm good bye to Francois, Katie quizzed Jeff in the elevator. "If Nikki is truly that ill, what happens to Francois? He seems very devoted to her."

"I'll have to find out. I'm sure he'll return to France to be near his father."

"I would, if mine were alive. Now, though, to change the subject, I know a really good restaurant about two blocks from here. We're already parked, so, do you want to have a very late lunch with me?" Katie thought of Harvard Gardens. Glazed salmon sounded good to her right then.

"Or an early dinner. How about that?" The door opened, and Jeff hoisted his computer bag to his shoulder. "Should we put this in the car?"

"In Boston?" Katie pushed on Jeff's arm and chortled. "Only if you have it insured. You keep that strap firmly wrapped around your neck until we head off to the apartment. It's got my house plans inside."

"Nikki's house plans. See? I was listening." Jeff's eyes twinkled. "Now, which way to Harvard Gardens?"

Katie pointed to the restaurant just across Cambridge, in dark brick, with a gold-lettered sign. They held hands as they made their way to a crosswalk and waited patiently for the light to change.

"Not quite like Rockhaven." Jeff rolled up on the balls of his feet, with a poorly concealed grin.

"It's not supposed to be like Rockhaven." Katie squeezed his hand and shook her head. She knew what he meant, though. However, you weren't going to get Harvard Gardens on the island. Sure, Harbor View was good, and the proprietors were warm and friendly, but the Gardens served up masterpieces, and at reasonable prices. Katie intended to enjoy this opportunity to the very last bite.

"Good," Jeff said, as the light changed, and they started across the street.

"Why good? I thought you'd want the rest of the world to be like Rockhaven."

"Ha!" he said, laughing out loud. "Then we'd be like them, and what would be the fun in that?"

"Come on." Katie tugged his arm, chuckling, as she opened the door to the restaurant. "Let's get something to eat."

"Hey, momma-to-be. Let me get the door." He leaned forward to take it from her.

"So you can get your food first? You have no idea how hungry I am." She let the door go, though.

"No, because I love you very much." He took her arm and insisted she enter first, whispering as she went by, "But I might give the waitress my order first."

"I don't think so, Jeff Ragsdale. Not on my time. This is my home turf. And for you, no lobster. You cannot order lobster."

He stopped, his hand on the door, holding it open. "And why not? I happen to like lobster."

"Because then you'd be like every other Bostonian on the street. Besides, I don't think you can get lobster here. Steak, yes, if you want steak."

"Then steak it is, my good woman. For you."

Katie, however, had her heart set on salmon. Jeff could have all the steak he wanted. Her stomach growled, and she didn't consider that the baby might be hungry, too.

This meal was all about her.

14

"Jeff, that was so much fun!" Katie closed her car door and looked up at Trinity Church, glad they'd found time to attend at least one of the Sunday services, albeit an early one.

"What's your friend going to say when she hears that all her secrets didn't stay secret while she was gone?" His eyes crinkled, and he fought to keep the laughter off his face.

"Oh, oh, Mary Allen's story about the foam reindeer berries, and to think Winnie tried to eat one—" Katie hooted with laughter and couldn't go on, because she was crying so hard.

"I don't think Rockhaven Church will ever live up to this. I might as well resign now." Jeff finally let his grin spill over.

"Resign now—" Katie roared. "Resign now, and

you can have—"

"—a position at Trinity Church!"

Jeff repeated the final five words with her, and by then, they had their arms wrapped up together, and it seemed they'd never be able to see well enough to drive away.

"Okay, that's enough." Katie straightened her back, and she wiped her eyes. "We really don't have time to waste."

"Because everything goes to waist!" Jeff shadow-boxed her arm, grabbing his stomach through his shirt as he pooched it out in a parody of a running joke that had consumed the Sunday school class they'd attended.

"No, I'm not going to laugh at that." Katie held a serious face for a moment before letting out a burst of laughter, then working hard to get it back under control. "Do we have time to stop by and see Nikki before we head out?"

They had, indeed, stayed at Katie's old apartment overnight, but it had been eerily uncomfortable. It was the same, and it wasn't the same. Then, Katie's old bed, and having Jeff there. It was odd, she'd told him as they snuggled under the covers. Not wrong, exactly, but out of step with life as they'd grown to know it. That morning they'd locked up, knowing there'd be no time to get back to the apartment. They intended to make the last ferry to the island, which meant getting on the road before noon to have a comfortable margin for possible traffic complications.

Nikki? That was a different matter. To see her,

Katie had been willing to sacrifice lunch at another of her favorite restaurants. Nikki was paramount, she'd told Jeff the night before, suggesting the early service to give them plenty of time.

"I didn't want to spoil your time at Trinity this morning. Between services, I phoned the hospital about a possible visit, and they said she had a rough night. They've given her a tranquilizer. I think seeing Nikki is out for today."

"I did so want to get back by." Katie felt the last of the laughter fading away. This was true disappointment. It wasn't easy to get to Boston from Rockhaven when you were tied to the ferry schedule. She had understood Jeff's infrequent visits before they were married. Now she appreciated the visits he did make. It was work.

"The good news is that Al called. The boat's not as bad as they thought, and it'll be ready on Wednesday. He said he'd run in with me to pick it up. How's that?"

Was that an answer to prayer? And how much was "not as bad as they thought"?

He took her chin in the crook of one finger. "I'm trying to cheer you up. How about this? I did see another restaurant I might want to visit. Since we can't spend time with your cousin, I think we can squeeze in a lunch date."

"Good. I'm starving. What did you see?" Something not too expensive, she hoped. His mention of the boat depressed her, reminding her of the job at ALD-Mass that hadn't materialized yet.

"Little Lamb. What's that, Eastern?"

112

"Asian barbecue, I think. Winnie brought home take-out from there once, if I remember correctly. They included a menu in the packaging. They have seafood, too." It pleased her that Jeff had suggested someplace, and the prices would be reasonable. She wanted him to enjoy Boston. It had been her home for the first three decades of her life. Of course she wanted him involved in that part of her, also. To make this dining connection, and at his suggestion? It was one more thing to bond them together in a life that Katie planned to enjoy for decades in the future.

"Do you think we can train Little Jeffie to love Asian barbecue if we eat there every time we're in Boston?" He started up the car, only to jump when someone knocked on the window. He rolled it down to greet Kambri Green, one of Katie's old chums from ALDMass. Katie had called her after they'd left Harvard Gardens the night before. She'd already had plans for the evening, but she'd agreed to attend services at Trinity with them.

"Jeff, Katie, what are you guys planning for lunch?" She had a long coat on, and fake fur around the hood rippled in the wind.

Katie called across the car, "Do you know Little Lamb?"

"Cambridge?" Street, she meant, but any Bostonian would understand that.

"You're welcome to join us." That was Jeff, with a smile.

"I'll have Harry. Is that okay? My sister's meeting me in about five minutes to drop him off for the day."

Katie laughed. "Yes, of course. Harry will have fun. We'll save you a spot."

Kambri waved and took off, fighting the wind. Jeff chuckled.

"What's that for?"

"The place looked really small last night. I hope they have room for four. Who's Harry?"

"Kambri's nephew. He's three, well, three back in the summer. Just watch what you say. He has a photographic memory. He repeats everything."

"Oh, this should be good. Like, I can train him to say 'Polly wants a cracker' just by saying it once?" He shifted into gear, and with a look for traffic, pulled into a lane.

"Don't you dare. Remember, you're a minister of the Faith." Katie held her fingers loosely covering her smile. It was funny to think about the little boy as a parrot in a cage, blithely repeating whatever Jeff thought up for him to say.

"And you're a minister's wife. You shouldn't be smiling about it."

That made Katie smile wider. It seemed indeed they were made for each other. She remembered an old rhyme one of her coworkers had called out during a very unusual shower they'd thrown for her back in September. Two little love birds sitting in a tree. Yes, that was Katie and Jeff, she had to admit, and she'd found the ditty fit like a glove. Perfectly, comfortably, and as if they were indeed made for each other.

"What are you thinking?" Jeff touched her with his elbow as he turned on the blinker into a parking space.

"God makes people perfectly, doesn't he? Perfectly for each other."

"I suppose so." He killed the engine and removed the key. "At least I feel that way about us." He tapped her on the nose with his knuckles and grinned.

"Good answer, Preacher Ragsdale."

"I love you, Dame Carver."

"Dame Ragsdale, now, you silly."

"Always Dame Carver to me." He hefted the keys, and he leaned in to give her a kiss on the cheek.

"For that, I'll let it pass, Otherwise, I'd have pushed you overboard."

"Ha! We're not on a boat. That says all there is to say about that." He opened his door, but Katie grabbed his arm, and he looked back.

"Then I guess I'd have to catch you before you hit the pavement."

"After we eat. I think I see your friend arriving." He pointed to a car pulling up across the street. The door opened, and Kambri waved.

"You get to sit by Harry." Katie let go and opened her door. "I get dibs on Kambri."

"Hey, I like kids."

Katie knew better with Harry. She was pretty sure Jeff would wish she'd pushed him overboard by the time they left the restaurant, but that was the way of things. She, for the next hour, intended to let Jeff babysit, and she and Kambri were catching up on all the latest news.

This was Katie's last lunch out for a very long time, and she planned to enjoy it very much.

15

"Archie's complaining about what?" Katie was preparing for the Love Extravaganza. It was that afternoon, and she was one of the servers. She'd pictured herself as an emcee, holding a microphone, and everyone else serving their children all their valentine goodies. It hadn't worked out as she planned.

Now she wore a white blouse and red pants, with long underwear next to her skin. Rockhaven was cold in February.

"The trucks coming in with the construction." Jeff was also donning his red and white. He'd agreed to join Katie as a "supporting cast member." Besides, he'd said, it's for an island cause. One for all, and all for one, or something like that.

"What trucks?" She knew what construction he referred to. The Point. With Nikki's funds, John hadn't wasted any time in putting his crews to work. It was only preparation work, though. Underlayment for the new foundation, she understood. How could that be a problem?

"Archie's a good man, but he has his days. It seems the trucks take up too much space on the ferry. He's had to wait twice, and I think it's gotten his gizzard."

"His gizzard?" Katie stopped and looked at Jeff, holding one long, white sock in her hand. She already had socks on both feet, but she intended to be warm. This was set number three. "Did I hear that correctly?"

"You heard me. His gizzard. It's that thing inside that grows thorny spikes when someone doesn't get his way. I think Archie forgot to have his removed when he was a boy."

Katie patted her stomach where it now protruded so that she could no longer hide it, saying, "You'd better not be growing a gizzard in there, Little Jeffie. No gizzards allowed in your mommy's tummy." Then she looked at Jeff. "You'd better not let anyone besides me hear you say that about Archie."

"Scout's honor." He held up two fingers.

"I'll have to get up to his place and see if I can smooth things out." Katie didn't want anything about her life here on Rockhaven to disgruntle the old-time residents.

"I've already talked to him. He, um, doesn't want smoothing out. He wants the trucks off the ferry. He claims there's a regulation he can pull up, and so on. I'll work through it with him. Tonight? You get to

117

enjoy your extravaganza." Jeff was dressed, and he picked up her shoes and carried them to her. "And I get to spend the evening with the most beautiful woman on the island."

Katie smiled. She enjoyed his compliment, but she didn't intend to let Archie go. In the next few days, she planned to search him out. He'd always been polite to her. Sometimes a woman's touch was better than the best argument in the world.

Before she could tell Jeff that, a huge racket erupted at the front door, as if someone were trying to break in. Faintly, they could hear Jeff's name being called repeatedly.

"I guess I need to check on that." Jeff set Katie's shoes down and headed out.

"Tell them we're not home." She followed him into the living room, stopping to slip one shoe on, then in a few more steps, the second.

Roker burst inside when Jeff opened the door. He was grinning from ear to ear. "Hey, all! Happy Valentine's Day!" He threw a handful of pink and white confetti into the air, and it showered over the living room furniture.

"Hello, Roker." Katie looked at the damage and shook her head. "I thought we bought that for the extravaganza."

"You don't understand." Roker pushed past Jeff and lifted Katie off her feet. He swung her around, while Jeff laughed, wide-eyed and incredulous. "It's Valentine's Day, the best day ever!"

"Enough. Don't forget the baby." Katie's feet hit

the floor, and she grabbed the back of the sofa to steady herself. She didn't want to be sick, not tonight.

"Why's it the best day ever?" That was Jeff. "What's happened to you?"

"Everything's happened to me! Jess has happened to me!"

"You're engaged!" Katie knew that had to be it. Since the first pumpkin pie Jess had sent for Roker, she'd known they'd get together. It just took time for them to figure it out.

"Almost." Roker's eyes were alight with energy.

"How are you almost engaged?" Jeff slapped his hands on his friend's shoulders, and he looked him in the face. "You are, or you're not."

"Okay, well, I'm not because I haven't asked Jess yet—"

"Well, man, why not?" Jeff shook his head.

"She said I couldn't, not until tonight." Roker moved his head back and forth in an aw, shucks, sort of way, and he laughed as if embarrassed to have to admit it.

"So you did ask her." Jeff was grinning.

"No, Jeff, I'm seeing this. Jess asked you, didn't she?" This was clear to Katie. Jess was a smart woman, and she knew Roker liked her, but he'd never cross that bridge without some encouragement. She must have asked him, just to prod him over the jump.

"Is it obvious?" Roker's words tumbled on without waiting for a reply. "She said I couldn't say yes then, but if my answer was yes, I had to ask her tonight in front of everybody. With a ring. Do you have a ring I

119

can borrow?" He looked at Katie with his question.

How could she say no to that? She asked him Jess' ring size, and he shrugged, but she said she'd take care of it. Now, he had to get home and get dressed, because he was handling the cookies, and the cookies went to the children; and by the way, congratulations, Roker. Jess is a lucky woman.

Roker's proposal that night took down the house, even outshining the auction and the prizes the parents passed out to their unsuspecting children. Well, maybe not in the eyes of Rockhaven's children, but to two long-term islanders, that one moment took the prize.

Just as Chipper Murchison moved in on the microphone as auctioneer, Roker jumped on the platform and pulled it from his hand. Jess was at the back with a pile of dirty plates she had collected from the tables. Roker cleared his throat, and when everyone got quiet, he called to her. When she turned to look at him, he said, "I got the ring, Jess."

That was all it took. Jess dropped the plates right where she stood, and she ran to the platform yelling, "Yes, yes, yes," all the way. It was her final leap that took down the house. She jumped into Roker's arms, and she kissed him until Chipper tapped her on the shoulder and suggested that it was time for the auction to begin.

Katie watched it all, and she wasn't a bit sorry to give up one of her rings to ensure Roker's and Jess' happiness. If they were half as happy as she and Jeff, it was worth every diamond and ruby in the world.

It was all about the love. Nothing mattered more

than that.

16

Katie's eyes were closed against the warmth of the March sun. It was one of those rare island years when spring rolled in easy and warm. Two days before they'd had snow on the ground. Now? She was in shirt sleeves.

She hoped the baby was warming up inside. He was out there enough to get frostbite when the nights grew really chilly. How could a child be so big at almost six months? To look at herself in a mirror, she'd think she was ready to domino right there and then.

A car door slammed, and she turned to see Janine's truck. Her friend must be on the opposite side. Being very short, Katie wouldn't see her until she walked around. The doors facing Katie opened, and boys started scrambling out. When Katie got to seven, she stopped counting and looked back to the workmen scrambling over the Point, preparing to pour the foundation for the new house, with the sounds of hammers and power saws singing in the sunshine. With the boys off for Spring Break, and the concrete work coming at the same time, Katie had suggested that Janine's boys might like to see the trucks in action.

There were a lot of concrete trucks lined up, but then it was a very large house. Katie thought of Archie Coombs and his thwarted ferry access. She hadn't yet been to see him, although she had made several attempts. He didn't seem to be available to her under any circumstances, and that disappointed her.

And now, seeing all this, she could understand his point. She also imagined he was especially irritated at the current crop of trucks that had filled the ferry today.

Out of the tide of yelling voices from the boys, Katie caught Janine's voice calling to her. Katie found her at the back of the pack, and she raised one arm high and waved.

"The old cellar." Kevie was first to get to her, and he stopped up short. "It's gone."

"What old cellar?" Tim Swisher, the boy who lived closest to the Peaveys, had a well-worn basketball, and he thumped it on the ground. Without waiting on an answer, he tossed the ball to Kern Pearsons, a thin, angular youth, whose white legs protruded from oversized shorts. He wore black socks and white sneakers.

"Turkey!" shouted Kern. He bounced the ball once, calling, "Tee," and, "Paulo!" before making a wild pass to Paulo Rivera, a blond, blue-eyed youngster who barely looked up in time to dodge the incoming torpedo.

With them were Matt Leaf, Jeremy Boggs, and Brookie George, the tallest of the bunch. Janine's three youngest pulled a remote control off-road vehicle from the bed of the truck, and the motor sent up whining cries of protest as they forced it all around the parking area.

"Space!" Janine reached Katie, and she spread her hands toward the expansive Point, indicating the unobstructed stretch of lawn. "Room to let the wild ones of winter roam."

Kevie hadn't received his answer, though, and he asked again, "The old cellar was too cool. What happened to it?" It was a smooth expanse of soil now, right next to the forms for the new foundation.

"They moved it over. See?" Janine motioned vaguely with one hand. "Go up there and look inside. That hole goes way down."

He did, and apparently satisfied, he gave a contented grunt, and he was off after the other boys.

"I guess you're the Spring Break babysitter?" Katie gave Janine a quick hug, and she laughed.

"Only today. I'd be out of my mind if I had these boys all week. Tomorrow it's the George's day. You want the other three?"

"One's all I can handle." Katie rubbed her stomach. Her back had started hurting, and at not even six months. She hated to think of how it would be at nine. She also held her sweater in her hand, because she could no longer tie it around her waist. She'd never considered the trouble of such little inconveniences when she'd started this process. Now, she was barely buttoning her coat. At least the warm weather was a reminder that it wouldn't be winter always.

Thank God for that.

"I expected the foundation to look bigger. At least the new location will give you better views out to sea." Janine had her arms crossed, and at a noise from the parking area, she turned to check on her three youngest, and she yelled, "No, you don't, Konnar! If you don't share, it goes back in the truck!"

"Mom!"

"Don't you 'Mom' me! I'm coming over there if I have to!" She turned to Katie. "I hope you get a girl. Boys? Oh, my heavens, who wants them?"

"If you think your race car drivers will be all right, let's head to the cabin. John can't be here today, but he said they'd begin to pour the concrete about eleven. I need to get off my feet for a few minutes. I also want to ask you about Kevie's birthday. It's in what, ten days?"

"The 30th. He's so excited to be a teenager. Al teases him that twelve will still be tweener. Poor Kevie." She didn't look like she felt too sorry for him, with the smile on her face and the twinkle in her eyes.

"What have you planned?" Some parents might consider her question nosy, but Kate knew Janine wouldn't care.

"A day off the island. Roker's promised to watch the three youngest, so it'll be just the three of us. I don't expect it'll be much except a lunch, although we

125

hope to get to Bean's and let him pick out whatever he wants, within reason." L. L. Bean's, she meant, the outfitting superstore. Their main outlet was a couple hours south, just close enough if they took the first ferry out.

"Bigger question, although probably a silly one." Katie had the cabin open, and she pulled two deck chairs out. The sun kissed one side of the wooden structure, and it would be warmer there.

"Shoot."

"Jeff and I saw Kevie walking to town a couple months back. He was carrying something, and he wouldn't let us give him a ride. What was that about?"

Before Katie had finished the question, Janine was laughing. "That, my friend, was a dead raccoon."

"No!" Katie's nose wrinkled as her stomach turned. To think, they'd invited him to carry it in their car. "Why a dead raccoon? What did he want with that?"

"Oh, he didn't. He just wanted the tail, but it was frozen, and he couldn't cut it off without taking the chance of damaging it. Keithie is a big fan of Daniel Boone. Al got him the old series with Fess Parker on DVD, and he watches it nonstop. Kevie's idea is to get his brother a hat like Daniel Boone's."

"A real raccoon hat." Katie chuckled. This was the best thing she'd ever heard, and from a real, dead raccoon she'd seen him carrying down the street. Only on Rockhaven, she thought. "When's the birthday?"

"June 1. He turns five. Kevie was lucky we had that snowfall, although he didn't think so at the time. It takes more than a tail to build a coonskin cap. Ken's doing the tanning, and he's using the rest of the skin for a full hat."

"Amiro? On Black Seal Cove?"

"Yes, the ones who helped with the auction back in February. Wonderful people. Private but wonderful, anytime someone needs a hand."

"Or a hat." Katie chuckled. The sounds of the cement trucks' engines revving up let her know it was time. "If we want to watch, we need to round up the crew. I'm told the basement walls will be first. Then they'll pour the floors. John hopes to take advantage of the warm weather and get it all done today. He makes no guarantee the break in the cold will last."

"Can't he insulate the pour?"

Katie looked at Janine askance, curious how she knew to ask that. She'd only found out it was possible after quizzing John about putting the foundation down in winter.

Janine shrugged. "Al likes home remodeling shows, and I do pick up a few things."

Sure enough, when they got close, they could see the forms lined with sheets of foam, labeled Polystyrene Insulation Board, on the outside parameters. The wall forms were filled with rebar, and looking inside, they were sunk far deeper than the ten-foot height that would make up the basement walls. Dotting the prepped basement floor were numerous holes that dropped into the ground out of sight.

"What are the holes for?" Janine pointed, as one of the trucks began approaching the foundation. "I've never seen that on the shows Al watches. Drainage?"

"Footings, I think they're called. They go an extra twelve feet, or to bedrock, whichever John found first. He promised me the house will never crack." Katie laughed at that. "It'll be an extension of the island, like a piece of the granite itself. Look. The trucks have caught the attention of the wild bunch."

The boys were running up from the shore, screaming to high heaven. Katie could hear them over the roar of the trucks. Kern had the basketball, and every few steps, he bounced it on the ground.

"Wild bunch! You're not kidding. Keep an eye on them. I don't want to go home and find I left one behind buried in the foundation. Unless he's mine, of course." Janine whistled loudly with her fingers at her mouth, pointing for them to go around, and five of the boys turned to veer toward where they were standing. On the opposite side of the pour, one worker could be seen backing two of them to a safer distance.

"Guess who I heard from?"

Katie raised her eyebrows. "On island or off island?" The machines were roaring, and they had to raise their voices to talk.

"From when we were kids. Guess. She was the beautiful one."

"Babes?" Katie couldn't think of anyone else who fit "beautiful" from when they were growing up.

However, Janine pointed to one of the trucks. It had extended a long pipe out over the construction site, and it ended in an open trough. Gray, wet cement was just starting to slide out. "We don't see that very often here on the island."

"Concrete trucks, you mean?" Katie pulled out her phone and took a picture of the mixture. Jeff would be interested in seeing it later. "Or new foundations going in?"

Her mind, though, was on Babes. She had existed in a world of her own, always wanting to be gone from Rockhaven. Katie had never understood that, hating the end of summer, knowing that she would be leaving it all behind for nine months.

Janine laughed. "Either one, trucks like this or foundations being poured. Babes, though, she's in Vermont. She and her husband run a bed and breakfast. She's Babes Fifield, now, and married to an ex-Army man. Her daughter's fifteen."

"Beautiful, like her mother, I'm sure." The only person Katie considered more beautiful was her friend Winnie, but then that's why she was in the field of modeling. It was a requirement in that line of work.

"I'm sure. That girl had beautiful genes, and I've no doubt she passed them on. I told her about you and Jeff getting married, and that there was a baby on the way. When I said you were rebuilding the Point, she promised me she'd be here for the opening day of summer."

"July. The fourth." That was something else Katie remembered. She'd always shown up in June, as soon as she could get here, but the official "season" didn't ramp up until the first of July. People wanted to be in place for the Fourth Parade that wound through the middle of town.

Katie wondered if the baby would be there by then. At her last prenatal visit, they had it pegged about the first of the month, but had let her know that it wasn't unusual for a baby to run two weeks over. Katie didn't want it to run over. She wanted it out and done with. Women in love with being pregnant? No, not her. She'd love the baby, but she was ready to sleep at night.

Then, when the baby came, she probably wouldn't get much of that then, either. Having a baby, she was discovering, wasn't a win-win situation. It was a "pick your moments to treasure," and let all the bad times go.

Letting bad times go reminded her. Archie Coombs. If her back kept hurting, she might have to get a lasso after that man. She had to administer some Christian love, and he was going to listen to her do it, if it was the last thing she did.

Unavailable. Ha! No one was unavailable where Katie Ragsdale was concerned.

17

"Thank you, Connie. I understand Mr. Hickox also intends to offer medical and dental coverage to his employees. If we can work that into the deal, how do you think ALDMass will respond to our application?" To Katie's job prospects, she really meant. She'd made sure the two were indelibly linked. They couldn't have one without the other. Then, she suggested, with multiple policy discounts, she might be able to get ALDMass a toehold on the island auto insurance market. With her on the island as a full time representative, that alone would be good motivation for people to sign up.

She thought it was working. She had no doubt that Connie was rooting for her, but Maine was outside ALDMass's target clientele. Upper management had to be convinced an agent this far north would earn her way, along with a good margin of profit for the company, to boot.

Katie just wanted a paycheck. Every week, every two weeks, or every month, she didn't care. An island boy had come by to look at Jeff's Jeep. He'd lusted with his eyes, but Katie had refused to let Jeff drop the price low enough for the boy to afford it. She couldn't tolerate the thought of seeing the Jeep on the island, knowing it was being abused by someone who had gotten it for a steal. Besides, Jeff loved that car. Katie appreciated he was willing to give it up for her, but she didn't plan for him to give it up at all.

Connie, she silently pleaded, come through for me. Now!

Connie left Katie on an upbeat note, telling her that with the new store policies lined up, as long as Mr. Hickox followed up, it looked like they might be shaking hands before long. She also wanted Katie to let her know how the progression on the renovation was coming, and she expected to see pictures of that new baby the minute it showed its cute little face.

Katie sent her love to everyone at the company, and she hung up the phone, very pleased. She had handled it all very business-like, refusing to call on any special favors because of her friendship with Connie or her past employment at the company. She hadn't known she could act as an independent agent, but she had pulled it off masterfully. Now, though? She had dinner to prepare, and little Jeffie was complaining.

Inside the fridge, she pulled out two covered trays. Jeff was so good to her. He was on his boat today, pulling pots, and he came in tired on days he fished. Yet, he went out of his way to gather the things for the next evening's meal, prepping the meat and vegetables so that all Katie had to do was put it in a pan and let it go. She had about five hours until she expected Jeff, and that was just enough time for steak, potatoes, and vegetables. Pulling the foil off, the steaks were trimmed and waiting, the potatoes peeled and sliced in half, and the veggies were rinsed. She dumped them in the crock pot Jeff had pulled down the night before, added two cups of water, and hit start. By then, her energy was gone, and she tossed the pans in the sink and headed back to the living room.

Her heart went out to Janine. How had she managed babies two, three, and four? Katie could barely get through the day with no children, and just one in the oven.

She must have dozed, because the next thing she knew Jeff was kissing her on the cheek, and saying, "Hey, beautiful. Dinner smells wonderful." And it did, meaning she had been out the entire afternoon.

"I'm sorry, Jeff. I must have fallen asleep." She started to stand, only to feel the tug of the sofa pull her back down.

"No, you don't. You stay right there. I'm headed to the shower, and I'll take care of the rest afterward. You're looking after two of you, and that's the most important thing."

"You lovely, lovely man." She reached for his face, to brush it with her hand. "I called Connie today. She thinks we might have a deal."

"A deal?"

That woke Katie. She forgot she wasn't telling him until it was certain. She used her elbows to force herself into a sitting position. "With Ritchey's new store. He asked me about insurance, and I'm brokering a deal with my old company. If it goes through, I might have my old job back."

"Katie!" He sounded distressed. "You don't need to work. We're okay on money. Sure, it's a little tight right now, but the Lord provides for his own. I've never had a bill I couldn't pay eventually."

"I love you, Jeff. Ritchey does need insurance, though, and he's getting it somewhere. Why not me?" She smiled at him. "Why else would our heavenly Father have sent him our way if not to help us out? Winnie meeting up with Ritchey, then Ritchey buying the store in town? He doesn't need this store to be successful. Trust me in this. Me, Ritchey? God's got a plan, and we're part of it, so plan to enjoy the ride."

"I don't know. With the baby coming, and the house out on the Point, can you manage both?" He held one of her hands in both of his, and he lifted it to his lips and kissed it.

"Oh, you are a male, to your bones." Katie was fully awake, and she laughed. "I'm a woman, Jeff. I can do anything. Haven't you heard Peggy Lee sing her trademark song? Or anyone that's sung it since?"

"But, I'm your husband. I'm supposed to support you."

"Support, shumort. I'm finishing up dinner. Help me stand." She held out one hand.

"If you're sure." He stood and took hers in his.

"I've been on that sofa for five hours. If I can't stand now, I'll be bedfast until July. No way am I giving up this early in the game. You, shower. Me? I'll have steak and potatoes when you show back up." Once she was on her feet and stable, she waved him off, and she headed into the kitchen, stopping on the way to rest her hand on a barstool sitting against the wall. Getting to the sink, she was aware of how braggadocios her remarks to Jeff had been. She'd been covering a gaffe, but he was more right than he knew. She'd felt pretty good off her feet. Walking into the kitchen? She already needed to sit and rest.

Well, she could do both. She pulled the stool up to the sink, and she nestled onto it. Flipping on the water to let it warm, she set the stopper in place and added soap. See? she thought. There are ways around every obstacle in life. You just have to find a happy medium to bridge the scary gaps in between. That's what Connie Rivera was helping her put together, a bridge, one that would help Jeff and her make it from year one to year two, leaping across and catching a falling baby along the way.

And if things didn't work out? There was always God's safety net underneath, made up of Nina and Kent, Janine and Al, Jess and Roker, and all their other friends on the island.

Katie was pegging her hopes on ALDMass, though. Insurance was her thing, and she could do this, no matter how many stools she had to line up along the way.

18

Katie stood on Neil Foote's stoop, and the soles of her feet hurt. The sun had been warm on the way out, but Neil's small place was buried against a moss-covered granite rise, a good eighth of a mile from where she'd parked her car. It was little more than a cabin with a metal stack and a stained propane tank off to one side. The towering trees kept the sun at bay, and the water washing the rocky shore not two hundred feet away had the rising breeze decidedly chilly.

She was here at Nina's request. Rather, Nina had told her if she wanted to meet face-to-face with Archie Coombs, then Neil was her avenue. The two men had a connection way in the past, although Nina didn't know what it was, but if one was having a cantankerous spell, the other could always get through.

To satisfy Nina, and to resolve Archie's differences with the rebuilding of Carver Point, Katie raised her hand and rapped sharply three times on the edge of the screen door. It banged louder than she intended.

"I saw you when you drove up. Nabbit, give me time to get my suspenders on." The words filtered through the thin walls of the old cabin.

The door jerked open, and there stood Neil, more wizened than old, with a three-day growth of beard, and still snapping suspenders onto the waistband of jeans that looked like they had seen better days in the previous century. He hadn't yet glanced up.

"Excuse me, Mr. Foote?"

"Eh?" He growled at the snap before finally clicking it shut. He lifted his head, squinting and working his face for a moment. "Oh, it's you. Let me get my teeth."

Katie watched him totter off, holding to the edge of a battered blue chest-of-drawers she could see just inside the room. His feet made a shuffling noise as he moved away. After a minute, she called after him, "I don't mean to be a bother, Mr. Foote."

"Eh?" He reappeared, standing deeper into the room. "Well, woman, come on in. Don't know who told you to call me Mr. Foote, but most people know me by my given name. Don't see how it should be any different for you. In, woman, and close the door after you."

"Thank you." She stepped through and pushed the door to, aware of the intense smell of wood smoke permeating the place. The woodstove looked cold, and there was an oil heater to the side. She'd seen propane out front, so there was that, too. She supposed he enjoyed having a fire most days in the winter. "Do you mind if I sit? I tire easily." She laughed nervously and patted her stomach.

"Suit yourself." When he motioned to her with his hand, she moved towards a chair. Neil was already in an upholstered rocker, one with oversized doilies on the arms. "Thought you looked in the family way. You the preacher's new wife?"

"Katie. I spoke to you at church." She was about to sit, but she caught herself and offered her hand to shake.

"Done know your name. It's my eyes not so good, not my memory. Wasn't sure you weren't that Amiro woman. Always coming by, wanting to help me out. Don't need no help, nabbit. I'm not an old man."

Katie wasn't too sure about that, but who was she to disagree with his self-assessment? She looked at her hand, and as it was still empty, she pulled it back and let herself sink into her chair.

"What'cha here for?" He began pushing with one foot, and his chair rocked. It squeaked, too, like a floorboard might be loose.

"Nina Vinson sent me out. My husband and I are rebuilding my grandmother's house out on Carver Point—"

"Eh, so that's it." Neil didn't let her finish. He stopped rocking, and he reached into his mouth and pulled out his teeth. He ran his fingers around the top where it fit against his gums, then he shook it over the floor and slipped it back into his mouth. "I told that husband of yours it was no business of that fool Archie. What's he want to complain about that for? When Old Mrs. Carver went, the man should'a let go, and he never could. Pardon me. I gotta get something to drink. My teeth make my mouth dry."

He pulled himself up with several squeaks from the boards under his chair, and he slid his feet towards a sink Katie could just make out on the far wall. She hadn't been sure it was really a sink before, as it had a gathered skirt covering the area underneath, and there were no other cupboards nearby. The tell-tale faucet, in battered chrome, gave it away.

He pulled a metal glass from a shelf attached to the wall, filled it from the faucet, and took a long draught. He returned the glass to the shelf and headed back towards Katie.

"What do you mean he should have let go? Did he and my grandmother have a falling out?"

He chortled until he coughed, and as he sat, he hit the arm of his chair several times until he got his throat cleared. "It was no falling out. Those two were in love, from the time they were knee-high to a root."

"In love?" Her grandmother had never said anything about being in love with a man on the island, and Katie had spent the first fourteen summers of her life with her. "My grandmother was Polly Carver—"

"I know who your grandmother is. All the boys on the island knew Polly Anne Ellison, or the lucky ones did. The most beautiful girl on the rock, and we all vied for her hand. Archie almost got it." His eyes twinkled, and he showed a liveliness he hadn't let through before. He rocked, too, faster than earlier. "Made him mad to come back from the war and find her married to that Carver chap, no more'n a rich summer boy. I done told him, over and over, no summer girl marries an island boy. It don't work out. Like marries like, and that's the way it is."

"Perhaps she didn't really love Archie . . ." Katie let her voice die away. This was a surprising side of her favorite grandmother she'd never heard about, and she hadn't known Archie existed until she'd married Jeff at the end of the summer.

"She did, and that's the truth of that. As I told Archie, like marries like, and that's what Polly did. Archie always hoped, after your grandfather died, but Polly was set in her ways by then, out in that big house, and even love couldn't cross that barrier."

"But if he loved her, why would he complain about the house being rebuilt."

"Now, woman, what'cha building out there? The same house?" He'd stopped rocking, and one eyebrow was askance.

Katie was startled by the question. "We can't. There were foundation issues, and a survey dictated a different design altogether. But why would that matter?"

"Archie's still in love. You building something that's not your grandmother's? You're killing her a second time. That's how Archie sees it."

"Oh, my word. I had no idea." Katie's eyes burned, and she glanced toward the door, compelled to find the man now and clarify the situation to him. "If I explain, surely he'll understand."

"Done done that. Nah, what we've got to do is get the man on your side. Think of that, woman. How we going to do that?" Neil began to grin.

"I don't know. He won't meet with me. He hasn't shown up for church since construction started. That's why I'm talking to you."

"Young people these days." He cackled. "That Archie, he's good with his tools. Likes woodworking. Likes babies, too. You might get to him with a baby, if you know where you can find one, 'specially one that needs a crib round about summer time."

"Oh, Neil. You are wonderful. Can I give you a hug?" This was going to work out wonderfully.

"Been waiting on that since you walked through that door."

Katie couldn't wait to tell Jeff. Nina had been her guardian angel, stepping in at just the right time, with just the right advice, and setting everything right. One thing she didn't see fit to correct Neil on was his pronouncement that like marries like. You see, on one hand, it was very true, so he was correct. Jeff and Katie were made for each other, as alike in soul and spirit as any two people had ever been created. Yet, Neil's statement wasn't true, either. Katie was as summer as they came, and Jeff was her island boy. She'd printed and framed that old picture Jeff had posted on Facebook, the one of the pack out digging for clams in the mud flats at low tide. Jeff, all covered with mud, proudly holding a clam in the air, and her, looking at him with admiration-filled eyes. He was her muddy island boy then, and he had been beautiful to her, and he was her handsome island man now. Yes, like married like, and no, like didn't have to marry like. It was, indeed, the love that counted.

She wished her grandmother had known that. Would her parents have been happier if they had been Coombs instead of Carvers? Her grandmother would have been, Katie was certain. Now, though, she suspected she knew why her grandmother had come to the island so early each year and stayed until the first hard freeze. She bet it was for love. Even if she couldn't hold it in her hands, to be on the same island with it must have been the next best thing.

Now, though, she had Archie to corral into her plans. A man that had loved her grandmother enough that he wanted to keep her memory alive, even almost fifteen years later? That was a man that any woman would want to know.

19

The melody was unmistakable.

The calendar had turned to April, Katie now drove with the steering wheel tilted as far up as possible, and the roadsides were littered with spring ephemerals, those first flower blossoms that would soon die back when the hardier summer growth took over.

Of course, a late-spring snow might kill them back even faster. Now, though, to hear *Oh, Christmas Tree* whistled along Main street made Katie's heart sing.

It was Jeff. Come May, Roker told her the song would start to disappear, but to Katie, it spoke of love, flyaway hair, and a wonderful lobsterman in her arms every night.

Today they were together to put love back on track for Archie Coombs.

"Hey, Katie. How's my little bump?" He kissed

her, and at the same time, he ran his hand over the massive protrusion that extended what seemed three feet in front of her.

"Your bump is fine. The bump carrier has swollen ankles. At the clinic, they said I was to spend two hours every afternoon with my feet elevated. I asked them if preparing dinner counted, and they laughed."

"That shows they find you as entrancing as I do. Has Archie gone in, yet?"

They had a scheme running. Archie had still refused to meet with Katie, and he had, indeed, complained at the town council meeting. To his frustration, his complaints had been taken "under advisement" and promptly ignored, but that had just made him more vocal. Now, Ritchey had been recruited to hire the man to do some woodwork carving in the new store, and they intended to corner him there.

Katie had her insurance proposals, already vetted by ALDMass, in a leather satchel to turn over to Ritchey. The reason for their visit was very legit, and there was no way Archie could fault their presence in the store.

"About five minutes ago. Are you ready?" Katie had been, but now that the moment was here, she felt her backbone softening. She was about to decide she liked the color yellow, and yes, to avoid this confrontation, she would replace her entire summer wardrobe.

Her eyes had even begun to burn.

"Not chickening out, are you?" Jeff squeezed her, and he chuckled as they began heading that way. "I see those tears. Archie's a pussycat. We both know that.

144

We just need to bring him around. Neil's idea is perfect."

"Okay." She took a deep breath, and she stood taller. "I'm strong. I'm a woman."

"Peggy Lee, right?" He chuckled again.

"Or Bette Midler, even Raquel Welch and Miss Piggy, once. I think one of the Judds, and half a dozen other people." She smiled. "The distraction is helping. Thanks, Jeff."

"Sure. Coming up, one hand-built crib on the way, Dame Carver." That was the plan, to get Archie involved in doing something for the baby, so that he'd feel included in the love he'd lost out on so many decades before.

"Ragsdale." She jabbed him with her elbow and laughed. "I'll never live down the Carver name, will I?"

"You laughed, which was my intention. Feeling better?"

"Sure. A kiss would help." She tiptoed, and he planted one on her lips. "Now, I'm energized. Let's hit it, Sam."

Stepping through the door, they saw Ritchey at the back wall standing before a large pad of paper hanging on two hooks. He wore a dark blue suit, with the coat unbuttoned, and his tie loosened around his neck, looking every part a successful businessman, instinctively involved in every aspect of opening yet another branch of a money-making business. He held a marker in one hand, drawing in a design as he talked. It looked like a shelving project. Archie stood beside him, in rougher

145

island clothes: a plaid flannel shirt, suspenders, and dark jeans that were too dark not to be new. His shoes were distressed leather lace-up boots with unevenly worn heels. A soft leather bag of tools was on a low table beside him.

"Ritchey!" Jeff called loudly and waved an arm.

"Jeff, Katie!" Ritchey called back, and he closed his marker and set it on the same table they'd used the first time Katie had visited the store. He put one hand on Archie's arm and spoke to him, before striding across the building, calling loudly, "Katie, did you bring those insurance quotes? My accountant needs to see how much damage you're doing to my bottom line." He laughed.

"Right here." She held up the satchel and patted it on one side.

"Oh, and do you know Archie?" Jeff took the satchel and headed back across the room. "Archie, this is Jeff, my very good friend from the island, and do you know Katie? She's been on the island most summers of her life. She's taking care of my insurance on the old place, here. If we go up in flames, she's the one I'm calling. After the baby comes, but you can see that, I guess." He grinned, backing away.

"Yep." Archie cleared his throat and kept his attention on the paper.

Ritchey winked at Katie, and he pulled Jeff to him, speaking with one arm over his shoulder. "Tell me about that antique crib you found off island. With my new godson being born in a couple months, I don't know that I'd trust some old thing put together with chewing gum and bailing wire. You say you can't find anyone to build you a better one here on the island?"

"We've been looking." Jeff made a sound with his mouth, and it came across as disappointment. "Now, Bean's has one—"

"Bean's." Ritchey slapped Jeff on the chest, as if to make him see the light. "That's the sturdiest you can get. How much to get it shipped up here?"

"Too much." That was from Archie. He still watched the paper, with one finger tracing a design Ritchey had drawn.

"What's that, Archie?" Ritchey called to him. "Do you have another option my friends could consider?"

Archie flicked his eyes to Katie for one brief moment. "That baby coming about June?"

"Closer to July." Katie hoped, just hoped Ritchey had broken the ice.

"Might could have one ready about then." Archie cleared his throat. "Good design here, Mr. Hickox. I never told you, but I knew your daddy. He was a fine man. I'll get you a quote for this." He rapped the paper with his knuckles and turned, reaching for his bag, and walked in a slouching clomp toward the door. He turned to look at the three friends just before he opened it. "Sunday, Jeff. Katie." He nodded and stepped through outside.

Katie laughed as relief poured over her. At the same time, tears poured down her face, and she tasted the saltiness pooling at the corners of her mouth.

"Is that good or bad?" Ritchey smiled as he looked between Jeff and Katie, with his hands in the air, and

147

his palms raised. He shrugged.

"Good, I think. Katie?" Jeff put his arms around her.

"I was afraid he'd yell at us, even after what Neil told me. I want to fit in and get along with everyone. This has been months, and I didn't know how much it had me stressed." She laughed, pushing away from Jeff and wiping her eyes. "Neil was right, though. You said baby, and he melted right there."

"I don't know about melted." Ritchey laughed. "I was surprised to hear my old man was fine. I didn't know Pops as well as I thought, I guess. My dad, a fine man. Two thumbs up, Archie Coombs."

"I told you Archie's a pussycat. See? I know my island people pretty well." Jeff pulled Katie to him and kissed her on the forehead before turning to Ritchey. "Thanks, man. You are the best friend I've ever had."

"Thank your wife. These are the best insurance quotes I've ever had. Oh, and Katie, I don't need these copies. My legal department contacted ALDMass directly last week, and we're all set to go. I talked to—" He looked thoughtful for a minute, then snapped his fingers. "—Connie Rivera, I believe, and she tells me you're returning to the company as, how did she put it, head of their northern New England division. She had nothing but praise for you. Let me be the first to congratulate you on your promotion."

"Jeff, you can keep your Jeep!" Katie threw her arms around him. "I have a job, now. We don't have to sell it."

"You guys!" Ritchey put one hand on Jeff's shoul-

148

der, and the other on Katie's. "With that house going up, I thought you two were set. I had no idea money was tight for you. Hey, all you have to do is ask. I mean, now that you're working, but if you weren't, I would have bought it and let you keep it, just so I could drive it when I'm here. Think about that." He thumped Jeff on the chest.

"Thanks, Ritchey." Jeff gave him a one-fist punch on the arm.

Katie couldn't say anything. She was too filled up with love to get any words at all out. Spring was here, the flowers were blooming, and she had a job. She had a job!

And now she had a crib on the way. What more could she ask for? Nothing, and to quote Neil Foote, that was the truth of that.

20

"Jeff, I need you. Let's go, now!" Katie was nearly in tears. She lay in bed, her stomach was so cumbersome that she could barely turn over, and little Jeffie had kicked constantly for the last twenty minutes.

And the sun wasn't even up.

"What? Is the baby coming?" Jeff jerked awake, and he fumbled with the bedside light. His clock toppled to the floor before he found the switch. His hair was a tumbled mess, and his eyes were swollen and red.

"I wish. Then this would be over. I need you to help me to the bathroom. I can't get up."

"Again?" He fell back onto his pillow, groaning. "I'm sorry, Katie. Of course. Let me get around there."

Jeff rolled off the bed and stood in a v-neck tee and

orange Texas A&M boxers, a gift he'd received in the mail from Ritchey. Normally he'd tout flannel pants, but this May hadn't exactly been normal. The first of the month had brought blinding thunderstorms they had thought would never end, even to the point of keeping Jeff off his boat. It had stalled work on the Point for two weeks, and with the thunder wracking her already sleepless nights, Katie had wanted to scream.

Then, the weather had broken, and she had sweltered.

Jeff had consoled her that the heat was the baby, but the skies had dumped unending sunshine on the island, and it felt like July. Hot afternoons were broken only by the grip of nightfall, when the heat eased enough to pull up a blanket for warmth.

This night had barely cooled at all, and Katie was damp with sweat.

"It's Rockhaven," she muttered, as he helped her stand. "How can it be hot at four in the morning?" The window at her side of the bed was open, but Jeff reflected the truth of the temperatures in his chill bumps.

"Here, beautiful, let me get the bath light." Jeff steadied her with one hand as he felt along the wall.

"Leave it off. I don't feel beautiful, and I don't want to see myself in the mirror. Oh, oh, hurry, Jeff. I need past now." Katie shoved him out of the way and scrambled to ready herself for her pending emergency.

That had been her nightly routine for the past week, and she was tired of it. Now, she lay sprawled on the sofa, the sun washed the inside of the room, and the sound of the ocean on the rocks lulled her into a welcome drowsiness. Anything that needed doing wasn't getting done today.

Her phone set off a chirruping sound. Jeff had reset the ringer, thinking this wouldn't disturb her as much as a rousing chorus of *Hallelujah!*, but it found its way in her head and jarred her awake anyway.

"Five more weeks!" She held the phone for a moment with her eyes closed, as it began its chirruping chorus once more. On the third set, she knew she had to answer, or she'd lose her caller. Looking at the display, she took a deep breath. It was Winnie. She brightened herself and tapped the phone. "Honey, I'm so glad you called. What's going on with you?"

"Hi, Sweetie! Guess where I am!" In the background came the sound of tinkling glass, like crystal tapping against crystal.

"In an airplane having lunch." Lunch. Just the thought of it turned Katie's stomach. Breakfast had not stayed down.

"Close. I'm in Monaco. Well, not in Monaco, but I can see it from my chair. Listen." Something high-pitched came through, falling off, then repeatedly rising in volume. "Can you tell what that is?"

"Um, your hairdryer?"

"Oh, you are such a goof! It's Monaco. Think that, and you'll know." She laughed, and she said something sotto voce to someone on her end of the line.

"Who's with you?"

"Stephanie."

Before Winnie could explain, the phone beeped

several times, and it went dead.

"Oh, Stephanie," Katie muttered, and she looked at the screen, shaking her head, totally clueless who Stephanie was. However, Monaco told her why she hadn't heard from her friend in the past few weeks. Glancing at the phone told her it was nearing eleven. "I might as well try for some food. Maybe I can keep something down."

She dropped the phone beside her and rolled to her side, crawling as much as anything to her feet. People from the church had been coming by to offer their help on a daily basis, but she'd told Jeff she needed one day to herself. She hadn't even had a break from the new house out on the Point. John had been calling regularly with updates, and there was always something new to put her stamp of approval on. She learned it was called a timber-framed structure, and last week, John had needed to know if she wanted the exposed steel joining plates painted black or shellacked in a natural state. She hadn't known what joining plates were, but she did now.

"Just tell him to build it," she'd told Jeff, almost in tears. "It doesn't matter if it even has joining plates."

He'd been more reasonable, assuring her that it did matter, and next year, she'd be glad she'd taken the effort to involve herself in the construction. He'd also rubbed her back, and they'd discussed how after several easy months of carrying this baby, it had decided to fight her tooth and nail the final six weeks. Jeff acknowledging that had helped. Katie didn't feel so alone.

About the time she'd waddled into the kitchen, the phone on the sofa started to chirrup at her yet another time. Taking a deep breath, she retrieved it to discover it was Winnie back on the line.

"Hey, Honey. The call dropped. Sorry. What were you saying?"

"Did you guess yet?"

"I think I said your hairdryer. Was that it?" She worked on the bright voice, hoping Winnie wasn't paying close attention. She didn't want to be forced to try to explain the state of her day.

Winnie giggled. "Here, talk to Stephanie."

"Bonjour. I am very glad to speak with you. Katie, correct?" The speaker sounded very educated and proper. A ship's horn or something similar went off in the background.

"Katie Ragsdale, yes."

"I understand you are having your first child soon. Congratulations. Do you know yet, boy or girl?"

"Thank you. A boy, we think, but we haven't been able to tell for certain. He won't turn the correct direction."

"Ah!" She laughed. "With my son, it was the same. Louis never did as we wished. I wish to express my sympathy for Nicolette's illness. She has been a close family friend all my life, and she is like a favorite aunt to me. I am so glad she shares her final years with her American relations. Give her our family's love when you see her next. Au revoir."

"Hi, Sweetie. I'm back." Winnie giggled. "Isn't Stephanie so sweet? She's let me come on her boat to enjoy some peace and quiet. Since you won't guess, it's the Grand Prix. Nobody can get a minute's peace in the city with those cars making noise all day. You can't so much as carry on a conversation at any of the cafés."

"Am I getting this right? You're in Monaco for the Grand Prix? Why are you in Monaco for the Grand Prix?" Even more, Katie was trying to place Stephanie. Had her cousin ever mentioned someone by that name, especially in the context of an old family friend? Not that Katie remembered.

"Oh, you know. Jeffie's friend." Winnie made a remark to Stephanie about something Katie couldn't see, and an air horn blasted. It was loud.

"What was that?"

"They have this thing called paparazzi. Everyone wants our pictures. One of Stephanie's little men is chasing them off in a tiny boat. Oh, this is so much fun!"

"So, why did you call?" Katie's chipper brightness was about worn to a frazzle. Her hunger was real, now, and Winnie's conversation was all over the place.

"Sweetie, I'm coming to see you, once my photo shoot is done. Ritchey wants lots of pictures of me with the race cars. I'm going to be a calendar!"

"Sure. You're going to be a calendar. And Stephanie? I can't place her. Is she the photographer?"

"Oh, Sweetie! That's rich!" It sounded like she covered the phone and told Stephanie Katie's question. "Katie! Stephanie's the princess, well, one of them. I bumped into her, all by accident. She asked me what the pictures were for, and I told her about Ritchey and you and Jeffie, and we became best friends. Isn't it funny she knows Nikki, too? She thinks Nikki owns an apartment here in Monaco. I knew Nikki had money, but not real money. Oh, Sweetie, how's the house coming along? Stephanie wants to know. She was at your grandmother's once, when she was a girl. Of course, you weren't around then, so you wouldn't have met her." Winnie let out another giggle, and she spoke to someone on the boat with her, although she didn't call them by name.

Katie sighed, her energy totally depleted. "The house is framed in, but the roof's not on, and there are no windows, yet. Tell Stephanie she's welcome anytime. Call me when you know you're coming in, Honey, but it sounds like you've got a lot going on, and I'm about to have lunch."

"It's dinner time here. We're eating on the boat. We have a real dining room. Who has a boat with a real dining room? Oh, oh, before I forget, here's why I called. I got a picture of me standing next to Princess Grace's picture. Stephanie took it. That's her mother. You know who Princess Grace is, don't you?"

"Grace Kelly?" It had to be. There was no other Princess Grace.

"Of course! I love you, Sweetie. See you this weekend!"

Katie watched the display on the phone return to its standard wallpaper, which was of Jeff on his boat, with a green buoy bell in the background. He wore sunglasses, and his hair was rumpled by the wind.

Grace Kelly, she thought. Cousin Nikki knew Grace Kelly, and she's like a favorite aunt to Grace Kelly's children. Oh, my. There was more to Nikki than Katie knew. And an apartment in Monaco?

Oh, my, indeed!

21

"Jeff, how was the party?" Katie was in bed with the covers piled over her. She had roasted last week, but this week she was freezing. Even though the phone had rung twice, she hadn't had the energy to answer it.

Winnie had been waylaid, thank goodness, in Boston. She'd stopped by to give Nikki a small present from Stephanie, and had called Katie to tell her there was a change of plans, and if Katie didn't mind, she thought she'd keep Nikki company for a few days.

Katie was grateful a new connection had been made, and she was more grateful she didn't have to entertain. She'd been ill the entire weekend. Now, she had doctor's orders to be off her feet at least one hour out of two. Actually? Three hours out of four was more practical.

"You would have loved it." Jeff came into the bedroom, wearing a bright tee with an ice cream stain on one sleeve, and baggy cargo shorts. One leg had grass stains down the side. He held a cell phone in his hand. "Did you survive all alone?"

"I wasn't all alone." She pushed the bedding back to sit, only to realize how cold it was in the room. "Aren't you freezing?"

"It's warmer in the sun than it looks from in here. I talked to Nina. She left the party early, and she said she'd stop. She made it, then." He leaned in and gave her a kiss on the cheek.

"She dropped off a pineapple cake. It's in the kitchen, and maybe a casserole. She tried to tell me, but I was half asleep. Sorry. Do you have pictures?"

"Remember that dead raccoon?"

"The one Kevie was carrying, the one we almost had in our car? How could I forget?" She smiled.

"Look at these. Keithie wouldn't take it off the entire time. I'm thinking I might have to have one." He chuckled, holding the phone out to her.

"Don't make me laugh." Katie was half-sitting, and she fell back onto the bed. "No, no laughter. That hurts my back."

"I'm so sorry. Is there anything I can do?"

"Not get me pregnant next time. Other than that, you're doing fine. I just have to get past the next month. Then I can give him to you and sleep in the guest room." She chuckled at that, wishing it didn't hurt so badly.

"I learned today why Winnie stayed in Boston."

159

He clicked the phone off and held it in his hand, looking at her.

"Oh? Because I was sick? There was no way I could have been a good host." When he didn't laugh, she knew. This wasn't good news. "What, Jeff? Tell me."

"Your cousin. We knew there might be complications from her fall. Didn't we know that, Katie?" His eyes had gone red around the edges.

"Spit it out, Jeff." Katie's stomach was a rock, and it had nothing to do with food or physical illness.

"You were so sick Winnie and I agreed not to tell you, but she stayed in Boston rather than coming up here because pneumonia had set in. I knew she had that cough when we were there, but I didn't think much about it. Francois called me—" He chuckled, wiping at one eye. "—and I had the hardest time understanding. That man needs an interpreter. Well, he called last week, so I already suspected something had happened. Then when you were sick in bed, I knew you couldn't go down. With Winnie flying in, she agreed to stay at the hospital with her. Even the doctors didn't expect her to go downhill so quickly."

"How downhill?" Katie heard the ragged edge in her voice. She couldn't help it.

"I'm sorry, my love." Jeff took her hand in his. "It was this morning, early. I got the news while I was at the party."

"No. Jeff, no. The house isn't finished, and I so wanted her to get to see the baby. No." She let herself sink into the sobs that rushed over her in waves, consuming her.

"Baby, baby," Jeff crooned. "No, no, don't cry like this. Winnie was holding her hand when it happened. The last thing Nikki said was how much she enjoyed getting to know her family again. She wished she'd done it sooner."

"I wasn't there, Jeff. I should have been there." She couldn't look at him, and guilt washed over her.

"She loved you, Katie. You loved her. That's all that matters."

"Did Winnie tell her about Stephanie?"

He wiped one eye and gave a snort of a laugh. "She said your cousin laughed and said she wanted to whip that girl once when she poured a whole bottle of Chanel in the bath. She couldn't, though, because she was a little princess."

"What happened?"

"When she found it didn't make bubbles, she drained the tub and came back with kitchen soap. She poured in the whole bottle and made the bubbles overflow the tub."

"Oh, Jeff. That's funny. She really said the princess did that?" Katie wiped her face with her palms. "Maybe we should hope ours is a boy. He might tramp mud in the house, but at least all my Chanel would be safe."

"I'd have to get you some, first." He took her hand. "Seriously, are you going to be all right? I'm sorry I didn't tell you. The doctors thought she was improving."

"Your decision was the best, no matter that I would

liked to have been there. I couldn't have gone down, anyway, and I would have worried. How is Francois doing? Did Winnie say?"

"Remember those file folders?" He smiled, but it was a wait-till-you-hear-this smile, not a real, isn't-this-exciting smile.

"In the hospital?"

"Yes. Your cousin was pretty savvy. The three we didn't look at concerned her estate. It seems she only has one living relation." He did the smile thing again.

"Who?" The question came out, but even as she said it, Katie knew the answer. "Sorry, but what does that mean? For us?"

He placed a hand beside her face, and he leaned in and kissed her. "It means you don't need that job any longer. And when we go to France, we can stay in St. Moritz or in your apartment in Monaco. Free."

"But Francois, what about him?"

"He texted me a statement the attorney had pre-pared. Francois will stay at the apartment in Boston until the estate changes hands. That timing is a little bit vague. However, Nikki did give him a permanent in-come, for either thirty years or life, whichever comes up first."

"I'm so glad. I really like Francois. I want him to be happy. I suppose he's ready to head back to France to be near his father. Good for Nikki, taking care of her driver. What about, you know, services and stuff? Should we plan something here, or will she be interred in France? Did anyone say?"

"France, from what the attorney's statement says.

Nikki arranged to give Francois power of attorney to handle her final needs. Your cousin was very thorough in her legal matters. Later, perhaps, we can do a memorial here on the island."

"I'd like that. I'll miss her, Jeff."

"I know you will, sweetheart. I will, too. Don't you want to know how much the estate is worth?" He grinned.

Katie sighed, and she looked through the windows out to Moffat Cove. "Will it buy you a new boat?" That would be worth a lot to her.

"A new one every year for the rest of my life. Do you think I need one?" He seemed very pleased at her question, and his eyes shimmered.

"Can I still work if I want to?" She tried to smile, but she wasn't sure what to expect. And she did want to. It was something she was good at, and she liked meeting people. She liked helping people, and she felt she was doing that when she helped them resolve their insurance hassles. One call. It was ALDMass' motto. She intended to adopt it as her own.

"You want to work?" He seemed puzzled. "Thanks to your cousin, you'll never have to worry about money again."

"But if I want to?" She felt her eyes filling up. "Please?"

"How can I say no to that? For the woman I love, you can work every day of the week, and I'll love you every one of those days."

Katie held out her arms, and even with the baby in the way, she pulled Jeff tight, and she hugged him for all she was worth. She might have cried for Nikki in there a bit, but it was all a package, filled with love, and wrapped and tied with the arms of a strong man who was hers forever and ever.

She was reminded once more of Neil Foote, who once said, And that was the truth of that.

Over the next four weeks, Katie discovered that her first trimester had been the easy one.

That ninth month? It beat her to death. Rather, it exhausted her, swelled her ankles until she thought she couldn't walk, and she only made it out to the Point once, then only stayed long enough to see that there were windows and a roof, and that the grass needed to be trimmed. She hadn't gone so far as to get out of the car.

Just shoot me in the head, she thought. Take the little stinker by c-section, and bury me in an old hole.

She didn't mean that, not very often, anyway. Then came the night she timed her contractions, to find they fit within the permissible timetables, and she felt the relief of the angels that it was here, and two days early. This was going to be over and done.

However, it didn't get better at the hospital. They knew she was coming up on her due date, so she was expected at some point. However, while the nurse practitioner was very efficient, an epidural was what Katie demanded. It was not to be so. He wasn't trained, he quoted, "in administering epidural injections under fluoroscopy." Katie wasn't sure what that meant, except that she would be screaming in pain for the next few hours.

"Winnie. Where's Winnie? She promised to be here." Katie squeezed Jeff's hand as a spasm coursed through her body. She was drenched, and she didn't know how pain could be so bad.

"She'll be here on the first ferry. She's on her way now."

"The crib. Did Archie finish the crib?" Another spasm hit, and she tensed, trying not to cry out.

"He thought he had two more days, but he'll have it before you get home. He assured me."

"He'd better. How long did they say these contractions might last?" She panted, and she looked at Jeff, jealous he wasn't the one going through this. She wanted to trade positions desperately.

"It's your first. They said several hours—"

"Oh!" Another spasm racked her body.

"Never mind. Not long, not long."

"Really? Not long? Did they really say that, Jeff?" She didn't want him waffling. She wanted him to spit it out.

"They don't know. Your first means they don't know." He looked like he might cry himself.

"You're sure Winnie'll make the first ferry?" It might be worth it if she had to wait that long. Then she could scream at Winnie, too.

"If not, Al's agreed to go pick her up in his boat."

"Tell me about the house. Anything. Distract me." When he didn't respond fast enough, she barked out, "Now, talk!"

"Um, we've got water." He hesitated, and when Katie screwed up her face, nodding hard and fast two times, he continued. "They put in a temporary sink, to put the well under pressure and check out the septic lines. Oh, and electricity. The rain the first of May means we can't be in by the Fourth, but it'll be weather tight."

"The fireplace. Tell me about that." She had her eyes squeezed shut. "Is it all river rock like I asked?"

"The fireplace is done, and the garage, it even has an opener. They have a toilet in already, so we have a functioning one of those." He grinned when he saw Katie glaring at him.

"Good." She spat the word. "I expect everyone we know to be out there on the Fourth. I plan to be there with this baby." She panted, as another wave of pain hit her.

"Breathe, Katie. Breathe."

"Don't tell me to breathe. Tell me about my house!"

"Papa, do what she asked. Don't stress out our new mommy." The nurse practitioner across the room called out his instructions with a smile. "We'll get that baby here, sooner or later." He handed Jeff a damp towel, suggesting he pat her forehead to keep the sweat soaked up.

Jeff had gone through a pile of towels, and a new nurse had come on shift, when there was a knock at the door. The front duty nurse leaned in, asking, "Visitors? I have someone who wants to come in."

Katie called out, "If it's Winnie, tell her to get in here!"

The nurse laughed, and in a few minutes, a familiar face burst through the door, with her hair and clothes swathed in hospital green. "Sweetie," she cried out. "Is little Jeffie here, yet?"

"You'd better be glad you made it. This baby's about to come, like right now." Katie spat the words.

"Now?" Winnie froze, as if seeing Katie prepped, Jeff at her side, and the nurse scrubbed and with gloves on for the first time.

"Yes, now!" Katie let out a yell, and Jeff's eyes grew wide. The nurse made a few coaxing sounds, and after a few moments, let out a sigh of relief, holding up a brand-new baby boy.

Jeff had just enough time to say, "It *is* a little Jeffie," when something crashed into an instrument tray, and they looked over to see Winnie, out cold, and on the floor.

"At least she got to see him born." Katie sighed. "Give him to me." She held out her hands.

"Dad still needs to cut the cord." The nurse clamped it off, and handed Jeff a sturdy pair of surgical scissors, as the baby began to wail as hard as he could with his little lungs.

"Wow, this is tough." Jeff sawed away, finally snipping it through.

That done, the nurse handed the baby to Katie, and stooped to check on Winnie before calling in the woman from the front desk.

Katie wasn't paying any attention. She only had eyes for her son. He was the most beautiful thing she'd ever seen. She brushed his face with her fingertips, and when she touched his lips, he hushed and began to suckle the tip of her finger.

"I think he wants the real thing." Jeff chuckled.

"My turn." The nurse stepped in, taking the baby. "I have some procedures I have to attend to, and then you can have him back."

"You did it, Katie." Jeff squeezed her hand, as his eyes tracked the baby in the nurse's arms.

"Oh, Jeff. We really did. Can we truly be at the Point on the Fourth? I want to show him off." She smiled. Pain? What pain? She had a baby. A healthy baby boy. That's all she could think of.

"It's only four days away."

"Four days. That's just enough time. Get Nina and Janine on the phone. They can plan everything."

"What about Winnie?"

"Oh, my word! Winnie!" Katie twisted around to see. Winnie was attempting to sit up with the help of the nurse.

"Did someone call my name? Oh, Katie, Jeff, I thought you were having a baby. I drove all the way up here. Did I miss it?" Then she caught the sight of the nurse sucking mucus out of the baby's nose, and her eyes rolled into her head, and she slumped into the nurse's arms.

"No, Honey, you didn't miss it by much."

Jeff chuckled and gave her a kiss on the forehead. "I love you, Katie."

"You'd better. I'm the mother of your child, and now you've got two of us."

Now Neil's words were really true, because her words said exactly what Katie really felt, except for one final thing.

"And by the way, I love you, too, Jeff."

Then the baby was back, and there was no more room for talking, not for anything except wondering how anything under God's creation could be so absolutely perfect; and to think, he belonged to them.

God's love child, wonderful in every way.

23

It was the opening day of summer, true summer, the one that started with the Fourth of July parade down Rockhaven's Main Street. The turnout was spectacular.

Afterwards, Nina had pulled together a fried fish spectacular at the Point, with a massive vat of hot oil bubbling away in the Ragsdale's new garage.

Of course, the house was unfinished on the inside, and the outside was rough wood underlayment, but all the windows and exterior doors were in place, and temporary stairs had been installed, allowing easy access to the second and third floors, to admire the views.

Babes Baker was there, as promised, now Babes Fifield, and she introduced her daughter, Wish. Why Wish? Because she got her wish when her daughter was born.

The surprise Babes brought with her was none other than Apple Dumpling, now married to Donald Crisp. Donald was at her side, red-haired and covered with freckles. He was a builder, himself, and he pulled John Chetwynde aside to discuss the challenges of home construction in such a remote location.

Apple introduced her three children, Macintosh, Braeburn, and Newton Pippin. All three were as colorful as their father.

Keithie Peavey ran the length of the Point over and over, his raccoon tail hat bobbing behind him the entire time.

Katie was surprised to see Winnie bringing a nattily-dressed man she recognized to meet her. She handed Jeff Little Jeffie, and she reached to shake. "Welcome, Mr. Sorensen. I'm glad you could make it to the island, today."

"Thanks to your friend, here." He motioned toward Winnie. "She has a gift for you. Francois!"

From beyond the gate, Francois appeared carrying a large item wrapped in brown paper. As he moved around people, he repeatedly called out, "Excusez-moi."

"Right here, Francois." Winnie called to him, snapping her fingers. When he set it down in front of Katie, Winnie ran her fingers down the fabric of his suit on one arm. "For one of these, I might even learn French." She giggled, reaching to brush the touch of gray that graced his temple, before turning back to Katie. "Now, though, today is yours. Your gift. From me to you, Sweetie. Open it."

"Jeff?" Katie called to him, but he'd wandered off with Ritchey, who had convinced his wife, Tricia, and their two eldest, Allie and Mark, to join him for the grand opening of the new store. The baby was back in Texas. Tricia had agreed, as long as she didn't have to get aboard a boat, not even once.

"Remember," Quincy Sorensen cautioned with a smile. "This is for decorative use, only."

As soon as Katie had part of the paper removed, she knew what it was, the old crib from the antique store. "Winnie!" She jumped up and hugged her friend, crying with happiness. "I love you so much."

"Then open the rest of it."

There was more, too, because the crib was filled with baby things. The best part was a doll, specially sculpted to look just like Little Jeffie. It had child-like hands and feet, and a cloth body, and it was exactly the same size. It was dressed in baby clothes and even opened its eyes when Katie picked it up. Winnie told her they had put it on rush order just for her, and Francois had driven it up from Boston that morning.

At one point, Ritchey was on his phone, and as he walked up to Katie, he clicked off and slipped it in his pocket.

"How are you holding up?" He smiled at her. "I heard you were under the weather the entire last month."

"Ha! That's the easy version. Compared to being pregnant, I'm peachy. What do you think of the house?"

"It's breaking my heart I can't get Chetwynde to do me a house like this in Texas. The views from inside are amazing. Enough of the house, though. We've one last gift for you today."

"Oh?"

"It's arriving now." He pointed to Archie Coomb's rusty old delivery van backing up to the gate, with puffs of blue smoke coming from the tailpipe.

"Archie got my crib finished." That had to be it. Katie was excited.

"It's more than a crib. You're going to need that big house to put it in." He chuckled.

"What do you mean?"

But by then, Archie was out, and he was pulling out pieces. Several looked like tree branches carved out of polished spruce, pale in color, with a touch of a yellow cast. Two large sections were carved into tree trunks, with roots that spread out to provide a firm base. The final piece he removed from the van was a carved ivy trough, with the ivy branches reaching up the sides to form an open fretwork of vines for the ribs of the crib.

Katie had tears in her eyes. She could see what it would look like set up, a vine-covered crib suspended from two trees, carved from the island's native spruce. It must have taken unknown hours to craft such an amazing masterpiece.

Jeff joined her on the way to look at it, and by the time they were there, Archie had it assembled. It was quite simple. They watched him set the two trunks in place, fasten the branches on top by means of a large, exposed peg, and place on top a leafy bridge that connected both trees. The ivy crib slipped in between the two tree trunks onto pegs shaped like small branches, locking the entire masterpiece in place.

"Archie, this is beautiful." Katie ran her hand along the carved leaves. The detail was masterful.

"I'm impressed." Jeff grabbed Archie's hand, and he pumped it. "You let us know what we owe you, Archie. Anything. This, I'm just amazed." He sniffled, and he pulled Katie to him in a hug.

"I never got to make one for Polly. Your grandfather wouldn't have it." He looked at Katie, as if embarrassed, and he cleared his throat. "I, um, helped myself. I hope you don't mind."

"No, I don't mind. Helped yourself how?"

"This is wood from the old house. When it burned all those years ago, your parents hired me to clear it away. I saved some of the best parts, mostly the floor timbers. I should have told someone, I know, but I never did. I've had 'em in my barn all this time. The insides were still good, milled from the trees right here on the Point. It's fitting, I think, for them to come back to their home."

"Archie, I don't mind at all." Before she thought, she threw her arms around him and gave him a hug. Hesitantly at first, then firmly, he hugged her back.

From inside the van, a familiar voice called, its tone as irascible as the man who used it. "It's about time the old grouch got a hug from a pretty Carver girl."

"Neil?" Jeff stepped to the back of the van. "What

are you doing in there?"

"What you think, nabbit? Old fool there wouldn't'a come out here if I hadn't'a made him. Someone's gotta light the fire under his breeches."

Katie threw her arms around Jeff this time. She laughed, telling him, "I've had the best Rockhaven spring there's ever been. I'm so happy to be your wife, Jeff Ragsdale."

"And I feel the same about you. Come on, Dame Carver, we've got a baby to show off."

"You, Preacher Jeff, need to learn my real name." She jabbed him with her elbow.

He led her to the new crib, and he pointed to the inside. One end had the name Ragsdale carved into it, and the opposite end spelled out Carver. "That's me, and that's you. Take one Ragsdale, add in a Carver, and that makes a pretty good baby. The best of both worlds, summer girl and island boy. What do you think about that?"

Katie didn't get to answer, because Neil Foote called from the van, "Young fools. Kiss her, Preacher. That's what I think about that."

Jeff did, and Katie did back, and if Jeff ever did want to try for a little Katie, that would all right with her; and that was the truth of that.

www.ingramcontent.com/pod-product-compliance
Lightning Source LLC
Chambersburg PA
CBHW070934250626
47159CB00009B/3238